The Worshipped Around Reality's Bend

Gods of the Flood

The Worshipped Around Reality's Bend

Book 2

Gods of the Flood

Copyright © 2024 by Clint Baker.

All rights reserved.

No part of this book may be transmitted or reproduced in any form by any means without permission in writing from the author.

Editor: Clint Baker
Cover Designer: Erin Diller

This is a work of fiction. Names, Characters, places, and incidents either are the product of the author's imagination or are used fictitiously. Any resemblance to actual persons, living or dead, events, or locales is entirely coincidental.

First paperback edition 2024

ISBN 979-8-3302-4028-9

Published by Clint Baker Stories
www.clintbakerstories.com

For Andrew

Had you not asked me about time, I would have forgotten a detail in this book.

Author's Note

Hello dear reader,

　　For book two, I wanted to focus on the development of monsters. My definition of a monster is a person who has lost their humanity or identity. In my studies I found that most monsters of mythology are either fauna or humanoid. In the fauna category I couldn't reasonably call them monsters because an animal from the gods would simply be another animal to them. Sacred or otherwise. I felt as though humanoid monsters were indicative to culture and were more so examples of the extremes in the human condition. An example being satyrs often represent lust. Because of this humanness I couldn't find myself calling them monsters. Afterall, The Baptized in Fire share many traits with humanoid monsters and I didn't want to take away their humanity.
　　I want it to be noted that monstrosity can be reversed through kindness and hard work. When I say "monster" I mean it in the neutral sense. The harm they cause and the ways they act are responses to what had made them monsters in the first place.
　　There are a few inaccuracies I want to address. In my research I wasn't able to figure out who the Egyptian god of bees was. I did find a single source saying that Neith was sometimes associated with them, however. I understand her mythology was completely different from how I represent and

I address this in "Flood War". The way in which stories are told with or without certain characters greatly influences the nature of Barrick's powers. I also had to change the timeline of a few myths. Some mythologies say that there was a war then a flood. Some say there was a flood and then a war. The rest say they happened at the same time. For the nature of Gods of the Flood I chose the latter. My theory for the discrepancy in events between mythologies and religions has to do with the time it took for civilizations to develop from oral traditions to written words. The closer a civilization developed to the flood the more likely the war in heaven happened before. I, of course, have no proof of this. I enjoy the thought experiment.

All thoughts and notions aside, I would like to invite join my thoughts and discussions on all of my socials to which you can follow at the end of the novel.

Thank you for reading,

Clint Baker

Contents

Part 1: Lost Memories
-Prophet of Eastrea   1
-Queen of Bees   8
-The Way the Tide Leads   15
-Colossals   30
-The Water God   39
-Monsters in Man   46

Part 2: Gods of the Flood
-Gods of Dust   61
-Flood War   78

An Immortal Tale
-The Book   125

Part 1

Lost Memories

Prophet of Eastrea

100 Years after War God

L**ouse clenched her eyes**. She teetered across Africa, looking for anything to take the visions away. She hated them. She hated how they made her feel like she should know what was going to happen but couldn't quite get rid of the familiar feeling.

She rubbed the images from her eyes again then stopped in her tracks. A horn like hers blocked her path. It sniffed her and shook its head. She put her hand on it. Careful to not spook it, she traced the skull of the rhino. It was content in the grasslands with no one daring to bother it.

"How did you get so peaceful?" She asked the animal.

"Not his time to be afraid," another woman said.

Louse turned to a woman with dark skin and deep eyes. Her wrinkles told the experiences she must have had in her youth. Louse wondered about the stories the woman could tell.

"Do not be alarmed, child," the woman said. "The Earth, she told me I would find you here."

Louse remembered Carca describing the Earth like a living entity. Could it talk to others like it did her?

"I would hardly call me a child," Louse said. "I'm older than you are."

The woman tapped Louse on the head, "But not wiser. My people know me as their oracle."

"Louse, Chris Louse," the Baptized said and then saluted.

The woman bowed. As she did, her hair grazed the rhino which sent it walking away to soon disappear in the tall grass.

Louse rubbed her eyes again. She saw the vast grassland turning into a barren desert.

"You seem troubled by your gift," The Oracle said.

"If you can call it that," Louse said. "It's more troublesome than helpful. I can't even control it."

"Let me see," the woman said. She stretched out a hand for Louse to take. "You are much like this rhino, child. Fierce and strong. But you need make a decision."

"What do you mean?" Louse asked. "I don't have any decisions to make. My life has been written out. We've made a complete new life here."

The woman gestured at herself, "Wise. I can see the future. In order to understand it, I must also understand the past. A trait you will soon have to embrace."

Louse blushed and gave the Oracle back her hand.

"You are brave," the woman continued. "But what you

have been through has weighed heavier on your conscience than you show. You need to decide which part of you to be. Are you your nation or are you here? One part of you or the other."

"I'm Eastrean," Louse said with confidence.

"Yet your face is from Earth herself?" the woman said.

"No…" Louse trailed off. She looked over to where the rhino had walked off. Her horn was identical to its there was no doubt. But she was born and raised on Eastrea. She saw the Earth grow and form to create such creatures. "I can't be like the Immortals because I'm not fully Eastrean."

"And you cannot embrace your gift because of the same," The Oracle said.

"What do you think I should do?" Louse asked.

"Chose!" the woman urged. "Will you be Eastrean, as you say, or will you be from Earth. You *can* be both, but you will suffer with those visions of yours."

The Oracle scooped up a handful of grass and twisted it into a ball. "Do you think that this grass could grow if it was sure it was supposed to be a tree? Do you think birds would make their nests with it if they didn't see it's potential?"

"I think I understand," Louse said. "Watch over me for a moment?"

The Oracle nodded.

Louse sat down, crossed her legs, and rested her hands in her lap. She closed her eyes and began to think.

Ration couldn't make us Immortals because we aren't completely Eastrean. My path is outside of Eastrea and Earth. Why am I here? A choice. Who do I want to be? I am Eastrean. I can work passed Eastrea. I was so scared. I think I was the last in a pod. No one else saw them all fall in the cracks. Everyone I knew gone... No. Later. I'll work it through later.

I am Eastrean. My home was Eastrea, my family was on Eastrea, and everyone I love and have left is Eastrean. I will remain Eastrean.

"I'm going to embrace my Eastrean side," Louse said out loud. "Nothing of my heart is saying to stay from Earth. I have no ties here."

Her horn felt heavy on her face for the first time.

"Oh. That's what that means," she muttered under her breath. "I need to give it up, don't I?"

"If that's what must be done," the woman said.

Louse drew her sword. She examined the sharp edge that she fine-tuned daily. Her reflection on the blade blurred her horn but was just enough to show her brown eyes.

"Would you mind?" Louse said, offering her sword to the woman. "It won't take much effort. Tristan is great at what he does."

"It would be my honor," the woman replied.

She took up the sword. Louse angled her face so that all that could be cut was the horn. The Oracle Arched back, and slice off Louse's horn with a single swing.

She barely felt it but a sting soon followed the cut. For the first time, she realized just how much was out there without having to tilt her head just to see around her horn.

The Oracle pulled a rag from her dress. "Here, child. It will need to heal."

Louse took it and wrapped where her horn used to be. "Thank you. I…"

A million visions blocked her sight again. This time though, she was able to make it out.

"I need to find Ration," Louse said. "Can I find you again? And can you teach me more?"

"I doubt that," the Oracle said. "I am mortal and old. The years pass differently for you. By the time you find me, I could very well be gone."

Louse's eyes watered. She took the woman's hands and kissed them. "Thank you. If I can't find you, I will pass on the kindness."

* * * * *

The trek was long but not as hard as the first time. Louse felt stronger and more in tune to her environment. She had a sense of the world as if it was guiding her to where she needed to be. The landmarks and paths clear in her mind.

It wasn't Ration she found first, but Arsenal. He told her about the new gods Ration had made friends with and the new love he had acquired. He guided her to their god as he told her about the previous battle and departed her once they found their god.

"Ration!" she clambered. "I'm so happy I found you!"

She ran and embraced the god which made the other beings watch in disgust. All except the woman standing next to him who smiled politely.

Ration hugged her back and put his hand on her cheek. "Louse, I've missed you, my friend."

Louse sunk into his hand. It was warm and comforting and—

"No!" she corrected herself. "I need to tell you something important. I have control over my visions now. I had to give up my horn and—"

"I saw that and have already healed you," Ration said. "I saw what you've been through. I apologize. I've been so negligent."

Louse felt under her rags, expecting the horn to be back. Instead, a soft nose with just the faintest tip was there.

"You couldn't have done that before?" Louse asked.

"You need have only asked," Ration said. "Your confidence stems from who you see yourself as. Have you met Calypso?"

Louse beamed and then saluted the Titan. She then turned back to Ration. "Ration, please! There's something I need to tell you… In private."

Ration motioned for Calypso to leave them. She kissed him on the cheek and glided away.

"You're free to speak, Louse," Ration said.

"I saw your future!" Louse said. "There was a war and you fall from some heaven and you were in so much pain and the other Immortals—"

"That's enough, Louse," Ration said. "I don't need or want our future. Let it happen as it does."

Louse stomped her foot. "Ration, if you don't listen to me, I will not follow you anymore!"

"Louse, I," Ration started to say.

"I mean it, Ration!" Louse continued. "I've lost so much already. I won't go through that pain again. There are other gods to follow now. If not one of our own, I can learn from them."

"I understand why you are upset and I didn't mean to let Eastrea fall as it did. I am so sorry for your loss. But the future is a tricky thing. I might know what is going to happen but I will never know when. Let us enjoy the time we have together, rather than be worried about the time we might lose. Does that make sense?"

Louse looked at her feet. Her new nose stuck out in her mind but wasn't as distracting as her horn was. "What would you have me do?"

"Don't tell anyone about what you saw unless they ask," Ration advised. "If you see something close, let me know. Then, and only then we might be able to prevent it. You'll be an amazing prophet, Louse. A lot better than anyone I saw on Eastrea."

He leaned in and whispered softly, "Maybe because you know how to listen and are brave enough to call foolish gods out of their heads."

Louse hugged Ration again. "I missed you. You know?"

"I missed you too," he said. "Now soldier?"

Louse snapped back into a salute. She pressed the back of her hands firmly against her weapon hilts.

"Go find the others," Ration said. "They've been worried."

Louse nodded and trotted away. She didn't let Ration see the worry in her eyes. He was so carefree and calm about the world. She hoped that his hearts could handle what was to come.

Queen of Bees

As the Nile guided him, Barrick became fond of early Egypt. The rich soil gave birth to fierce and magnificent creatures that captured his attention.

On one particular day that he didn't feel was as important as it was, he felt a strange sense of familiarity on the river's banks. As he approached the spot, he heard a soft hum. It was clearly a woman who paid him no attention.

Her long, black hair was tied up so that it was out of the way of her fingers at work on her loom. She was only halfway done with it but the design showed crocodiles and fish swimming together.

"It's beautiful," Barrick said.

"Yes, well... I've had a lot of practice so it should be," the woman said. She twisted her thread to begin a new line. The bees and flowers danced across the bottom with an empty canvas over half of the way empty. Barrick watched until she designed a stinger for the next bee.

"I'm not as good but I do something similar," Barrick pulled on the threads of reality. With some effort he was able to weave a small patch of reeds into existence.

"Amazing in its own right," the woman said. She didn't look away from her loom.

"Oh," Barrick said. "Can I ask your name? I'm Barrick Teal, Immortal of Reality."

The woman stopped for a moment to look Barrick over. As she turned, Barrick saw a bow and set of arrows at her side. She decided that the man was harmless enough and said, "Neith. I'm a goddess of war."

"Amazing," Barrick said. His eyes lit up at her name.

Neith rolled her eyes but smiled none the less. She went back to her loom.

"Can you teach me to weave like that?" Barrick asked.

"You shall," she said, motioning for him to sit next to her. Barrick lifted his hands to follow her motions.

Just then, a bee landed on each of his fingertips. They clung to him like they were trying to become part of his fingers. He paused and set them onto the reeds he created moments ago.

"They like you," Neith noted with an amused smile.

"Oh, the bees?" Barrick agreed. "Yeah, I like them too. They seem calm when around me so I let them do as they please."

Neith lowered her hands and stared at him. Who was this curious man? Why did she feel so at peace next to him?

An image caught their eye. It was a shadow running across the bank with a sense of urgency that made Neith tilt her head.

"Later than normal," Barrick said as he watched it too. "Arsenal has been across the Mediterranean for little over a month now. It really needs to learn to keep up."

Neith turned to Barrick, "You lead a strange life."

Barrick laughed, "I suppose you're right."

"Can I show you something?"

"Of course," Barrick said with such excitement that it made Neith wonder what else made Immortal smile.

She guided him around a bend in the river. Above its banks where the water wouldn't get to them when the floods came, were six bee hives. They were clay tubes on a clay platform. Bees flew in and out as they gathered ingredients for their honey.

When they were closer, bees flew up to Barrick. They buzzed happily in his ear to tell them about their day. He would nod and tell them how amazing each story that was near the same to each other was. Some rubbed on his cheeks then flew away back to work. Others seemed to greet him and did the same

"You get along well with them," Neith said.

"I like bees," Barrick said. "They're incredibly important in the world I built for everyone. Sure, other insects help but bees are my favorite. Most of them are just so happy that it isn't too difficult to love them."

Neith laughed, "Most?"

"Well, some are really angry. I don't know why that is." Barrick looked confused and thoughtful. Neith thought he might add onto the thought but he just scrunched his face more until a bee landed on his nose. It danced a message to him before flying off.

"What did that one say?" Neith asked.

"He thinks the queen is the best part of the hive," Barrick translated. "So dedicated."

Neith laughed. Her eyes squinted as she did so. She covered her mouth with her finger tips doing little to hide her broad smile.

Barrick found himself staring at it. He couldn't help but feel lost in the beauty of the smile that made his heart nearly stop.

"Can I show you something as well?" Barrick asked.

"Of course," Neith sad, enthusiasm seeping from her eyes.

* * * * *

"It's so amazing!" Neith cheered. She had set her bow down inside the last door of Reality's Bend. Her bare feet glided across the grassy fields.

Barrick watched on his hill. He changed the scene from snow, to fog, to bright and sunny.

"And you made this place? You can do anything here?" Neith asked.

"Of course!" Barrick said. "It's technically my mind. It filters as I need to make sure reality stays in check."

"I love it!" Neith screamed. Her echoes filled the thought bubble. "Empty. Barrick? Can we make something together?"

He slid down the hill next to her. "I don't see why not."

"Okay!" She clapped her hands and took his. "I want you to look into my thoughts and see what I was thinking."

Barrick did as she said. He saw a small building with

wooden planks and a straw roof. When he opened his eyes, they were in the hut. It had no decorations. Nor anything remarkable other than it would function as needed.

He looked around it and tried to figure out why she wanted the nicety.

"It's something we can do together!" she said. "We can come here and see what we can make. It'll be like a little workshop. With a table for drafting here."

A table popped up where she pointed.

"And a resting station here," She continued. A chair and bed popped up where she pointed. Beside the chair there was a water vase handy.

"Making roots, huh?" Barrick laughed.

Neith blushed. "If that's okay with you. And if we have time. My children and I are important in these lands. But I would love to be back!"

"I can't wait," Barrick smiled.

"Neith!" a harsh voice echoed from outside Reality's Bend. "Neith come out here! We do not associate with false gods!"

"I'm an Immortal," Barrick complained.

"Oh Set," Neith said, shaking her head. "We better talk to him."

On the way out, Neith was sure to grab her bow. Without drawing it back, she nocked an arrow on the string. Barrick materialized a sword and shield to follow suit.

Set's long nosed, dog like head glared down at them. "We do not mingle with forgotten gods."

"Oh, blazes, what's my name?" Barrick said.

Neith giggled at him which made him share a stupid grin.

"Worthless god with no people," Set said.

"Why are you here, Set?" Neith complained. "I haven't done anything wrong."

"I told you. We do not mingle—," Set said before being interrupted by Neith.

"We do not mingle with forgotten gods," Neith finished. "Though *this* Immortal will definitely be remembered."

"Are you coming or not?" Set asked. He slashed his hand down and a weapon with a spike at a "V" materialized.

Neith nocked an arrow and aimed it at Set's eye. "I doubt you're faster than me."

Barrick read the both of them. He saw their hostility and their power growing as they prepared to fight. He materialized his sword at his back. His plan was to wait for Neith to fire, then use that time between then and Set making his move to slide around her and cut upwards. A plan he didn't get to try.

Bees joined them all. They swarmed around Neith and Barrick, but not landing on them. One flew up to Set's face. It tried to land on him but he brushed it away. Angered, it dove down and stung him on his nose.

Set yelped and rubbed the sting. Taking their cue, the other bees swarmed the god. They stung at him, making him take his attention away from Neith and Barrick. Set swiped at the swarm, backing away. Defeated, he disappeared in a puff of smoke.

"Bit angry, isn't he?" Barrick joked. The image of War god popped into his mind. The scowls between the two were identical.

"He'll get over it," Neith said.

They stared at each other for a second. Neith glanced up at Barrick's hair which was more or less ruffled in the front.

"Same thing tomorrow?" she asked.

"I can't wait," he replied.

Neith put a hand on his chest and kissed him on his cheek. "Tomorrow then."

She backed away and disappeared, leaving behind the smell of river water. Barrick placed his hand on his cheek. For the first time since his creation, he became conscious of the passage of time so he would not miss a single moment.

The Way the Tide Leads

The Reacher swayed against the air currents. It was tough work, but Kataract managed to keep the sails at just the right angle to stay in the sky.

Barrick and Neith accompanied him on his journey to the far reaches of India. He watched them as they bonded around the deck.

Barrick lifted his shirt and squeezed his belly button. In a strange and deep voice, he said, "Neith very pretty."

Neith laughed and in the same manner said, "Barrick very handsome. Would like kiss."

They then made "Muah" noises as they touched bellies.

Realizing they were being watched, they turned to Kataract who only raised an eyebrow. Unbothered, they burst into laughter and continued with their antics.

Gods of the Flood

Kataract was unnerved by what constituted as fun to the couple, but he also felt a great longing in his heart. He reminisced about how he used to spend quality time with his own wife. He sighed. In his thoughts, he let The Reacher slip. He snapped back and pulled so that all he had left from Eastrea was back on course.

"Are you well, Kataract?" Neith asked the Immortal of Currents.

"Yes, I was just lost in thought," he replied.

"Is there a map for that?" Neith asked.

"I like that idea," Barrick said.

Neith winked at him.

"I think we should dock soon," Kataract said. He scanned the clear sky. A bushel of clouds greeted them as they encroached on the new land. "I think I'm about to lose my current."

"Need me to guide you?" Barrick asked.

"No, I see a good spot."

The captain loosened the top of his sails so that they started to descend. He twisted and let the currents guide them until they departed all together, leaving the immortals almost stranded on the Indian mountain side. They could hear the birds below them. They glided, much like The Reacher, between branches. Their songs carried for miles. Happy chirps that called to the innermost workings of the world.

Kataract checked the clouds he saw before. They were stationary. He then scanned the tops of the trees but they too, were idle. Only monkeys shook them in an attempt to taunt predators.

"How long do you think?" Barrick asked.

"A few hours at the most," Kataract said. "I'm thinking

that it will be much less."

"Barrick!" Neith gasped. "A honey bee!"

Barrick shot up and ran to her. It was collecting nectar from an orange flower with a darker orange center.

"He's happy!" Barrick said. It shook with enthusiasm as it gathered all it could.

"We should gather some for Reality's Bend," Neith said. "I think they'll do well there."

"We'll have to make sure they're healthy so they don't bring anything to the others but that's a good idea."

She gave him a quick kiss and went back to watching the bee.

Barrick felt a tinge on the back on his neck. Without saying a word and making it obvious, he tapped Neith's knee as he stood up. He stretched his back and searched for the owner of the eyes that were watching them.

Kataract noticed too. He kept at work pulling The Reacher's ropes back to take off position. As he did, he was sure to step within reaching distance of his crossbow. Tristan had made several modifications to it so that it fired at a higher rate and used less air as it gathered materials. The bolts that used to be nearly a foot long were now no longer than a finger but were just as deadly.

Barrick turned to Kataract. He mouthed *talk* and Kataract nodded.

"We know you're here," Barrick said. Neith stood at his back. Had she heard the music that came from Barrick when he was ready for a fight, she would have drawn her bow. "Come out."

"Your senses are strong," a woman's voiced cackled. She flew up and landed between the two Immortals. The woman was more bird than person. She was suited in elaborate armor decorated with elephants and the gods of the lands. Her bird head held tight, bright red feathers and equally magnificent wings. She towered over them by a foot and a half. "I smell someone serpentine on you. I wonder if you would taste the same."

"We are just passing through," Kataract said.

The bird woman snapped her neck at the captain. "Is that so?"

Neith listened to Barrick. She heard a dull, *thud thud thud*, which was just as likely to be his heart beat as the first drums of a fight.

The bird woman looked around Kataract and lowered her guard. "How did you get this boat up here? It's much too large to pull it up from the river."

"You didn't see us fly in?" Kataract asked.

"Fly, ha!" the bird woman said. Her laughter was like a chicken enjoying its day. "*I* fly foreigners. Boats do not."

"Well, technically Ra's ship flies too," Neith said. "He and Set are really good at it."

"Who?" the bird woman asked with genuine curiosity. She hadn't drawn a weapon yet. Barrick read no hostility in her, rather a coy sense of humor that took joy in making people uncomfortable.

"A friend of ours," Barrick said. "I'm Barrick, the Immortal of Reality. This is my love, Neith. The dark man with the large folded hat is Kataract, the Immortal of Currents. We really didn't mean to trespass. Who are you?"

"Asha," she said. "A karura and your escort."

"Escort?" Barrick noted. "By your expression you just happened upon us."

Asha ruffled her feathers, "Well I knew something might be wrong this way. I don't have the station to make a judgment about you three. Please come quietly."

"Coincidence is the language of reality," Barrick said. He glanced at Kataract for guidance but the immortal only shrugged. "Can you guarantee our safety?"

Asha leveled her eyes at the Immortal of Reality, "I get the feeling it is *I* who should be worried about my own safety."

Neith knew exactly what the bird woman was talking about. When she first met Barrick, she knew he was one of the most powerful beings in the universe. His kindness was pure luck.

"We'll go with you," Kataract said. "After all, friendship only happens when you meet the other."

Asha bowed her head and motioned for the trio to follow. She found a level clearing and looked to the sky.

"This should be good," she said. She reached out a hand and motioned for the others to take.

Kataract went to grab for it, then felt a slight harsh breeze on his back. He grabbed Neith by her hip and kicked Asha, sending the three flying.

Barrick, confused by the quick action, didn't move. His eyes drifted around them, trying to see what Kataract was reacting to. The effort was too little. That breeze turned into a gust and a new god tore his hand into Barrick's chest.

The god ripped it out, making Barrick buckle to his knees.

"Barrick!" Neith yelled. She tried to squirm free but Kataract's firm grip wouldn't let her.

"What are you doing?" the god snapped at the Karura.

"Taking them to lord Indra," Asha said, bowing to the god.

Neith stared at Barrick. She didn't allow herself to shed tears in front of these new beings. Then she saw Barrick lift his hand to his chest.

"You would put our home in danger?" Vayu scolded.

"They seemed friendly," Asha tried to defend herself.

"And you didn't think to question them further? Are you that ignorant of the times we live in?"

"I thought we were supposed to love and give welcome to others," Asha said, bowing lower.

"Your presentation didn't tell us that," Kataract said under his breath.

"Not other deities," Vayu said. He would have argued more but a sword tip cut up at him. The god swung back at Barrick, but found it hard to focus. The Immortal slid under the god's arms and put himself at a safe distance. "I thought I killed you."

"You missed," Barrick said. Power leaked from his words like a soft melody.

Vayu looked at his hand, then showed Barrick. "I have your blood on my hand."

"Yet I have no wound," Barrick showed where the god thought he had struck him.

"I struck you, I felt it."

"What is the probability that you did?" Barrick toyed. "You have blood on your hand, but it can't be mine. I have no wounds."

The god sniffed his hand. Now that they had some distance, Barrick took in the god. Vayu stood another foot above Asha. The flag at his side had two triangles that pointed the opposite way that the wind god faced. His body was decorated in intricate jewelry and tightly woven robes. Atop his head was a sort of golden crown that twisted up to a peak like a mountaintop. Barrick made a note to find out what it was called later.

"I struck your lungs," the god said. "I stole your breath."

"Do I need to do such a thing?" Barrick countered. "Seems like a silly waste of time."

Neith, relieved at Barrick's good health, grinned at the god's confusion. She forced Kataract to let her go and drew an arrow. "Let us go. We were only passing through and marveling at your lands. We didn't want any trouble."

The god turned to the goddess. "You've trespassed without proper means. Why should we let you go?"

"Because we caused no harm until you showed up," Barrick said. "Even then, I missed."

"Neither did I... Apparently," Vayu said. He analyzed his blood-soaked hand. Who were these beings? He could tell that the goddess was his equal in power but the other two far outclassed him. Age wrinkled their eyes in ways he could only hope to achieve.

"Barrick," Kataract whispered. "Take Neith and get out of here. I think I'm going to explore these lands for a while."

"How do you propose I do that?" Barrick whispered back.

"I know you have your ways," Kataract said. "And I have mine. I'm going to see what kind of trouble I can get into. Besides, you're not the only one who has picked up a few tricks."

"On your mark then," Barrick said.

"Right," Kataract said. He took a deep breath. He blinked hard so that his eyes were clear. "Now."

Barrick charged. He jabbed at the wind god. Vayu leaned away from him. Kataract drew his sword and swiped from behind his fellow Immortal. The god sent a gust to throw the sword down.

Vayu kicked Kataract's sword to throw him off balance. Barrick swiped in an arc but Vayu slid away. This left an opening for Kataract who brought his sword against the god's flag.

Barrick, seeing his chance, dove for Neith who was putting herself at the Immortals backs.

In the moment where the Immortal of Reality and the Egyptian goddess were out of the visual plane of all creatures present, they grasped each other's hands and disappeared under the probability that they were never there.

"A sacrifice?" Asha asked.

"Hardly," Vayu said. "You don't like showing off."

"I don't like being the center of attention," Kataract said. He formed a wind current under his palm and let it tear away at Vayu who pushed it up with his own.

Vayu swiped his flag at Kataract, sending a flurry of dust and leaves. Kataract formed a tiny tornado around him that lifted him up and ate the god's wind.

"What kind of power do these two have?" Asha asked. She felt the air in her chest starting to leave her as the two deities gathered the wind around them. "I need to get to safety."

She glanced over to the Reacher. Its sails were up as it waited to be commanded. She bolted for it before the harsh winds could start tearing away at her.

Clint Baker

* * * * *

Barrick and Neith rolled behind Sark. They shot up with their fists ready for who was trying to take them.

With a sigh of relief, they signed, "Barrick? A warning would be appreciated!"

"Is there anyone near Kataract?" Barrick gasped.

Sark listened for a moment. Through closed eyes, Sark could make out Kataract's fight. Then the familiar grunts of someone pushing through trees down the mountain.

"As it so happens, someone is close," Sark signed.

"Send them," Barrick said.

Puzzled, Sark stepped away to send a voice to their friend's head.

Barrick turned to Neith. Before he was able to get a word out, she hugged him tight. "I thought you died."

He kissed her head, "Hey, I'm not going anywhere. I promise."

"We could have stayed," Neith said. She nestled her face where she saw Barrick get struck. "Why did we run."

"The Eastreans don't have land to reside over," Barrick said. "No people, no resources, nothing. You could have taken him, easy. But had you killed him, or he killed you, either side would have started a war that would tear apart all lands in between. He'll be fine. Don't worry."

"We still could have done something," Neith whispered. She tried to bury her head deeper into his chest.

"I know," Barrick said. "Kataract can take care of himself. He's in his element after all."

Gods of the Flood

* * * * *

Kataract swiped down with a new air current. Vayu was able to deflect most of it into the trees and rocks behind him. They split open to tumble away from the fight.

"Getting nervous?" Vayu asked as he made a gust push forward. "Maybe you should have allowed your friends to stay. They seemed at least a little competent."

"More than so," Kataract said. He grinned with pride. "Blazes, they were pushing me to insanity on the way here. I didn't want to deal with them on the way back."

Vayu planted his feet and tilted his head. "Why?"

"They're in love," Kataract laughed. "Disgustingly so."

"Hm." Vayu grunted. "I thought they were an odd couple."

"Completely," Kataract agreed. "But amazing none the less. Say, you wouldn't want to part ways, would you?"

"I'm afraid I can't," Vayu admitted. "I must defend my home. And you new beings are threats to our people."

"I'm older than you," Kataract countered. "I promise you."

"I find that hard to believe," Vayu said. "My people created the universe and all those in it. I think I would remember if it mentioned someone like you. Despite you looking quite similar to us."

"I watched this planet form and helped it create the life that made you, I'm older," Kataract urged.

"And I have no memory," Vayu said. "I respect you. But I must do what I have to. To protect my people."

"So be it," Kataract said. He readied his sword in the

same way Vayu did his.

Vayu went to send another air current but was caught by the neck by an enormous form. It gripped him tight with his trunk. It swirled him around and slammed the god into the ground.

"Ganesha?" Vayu gasped. "What are you doing?"

"Ganesha?" the figure asked. He pounded his chest with his shield hand. The shield itself was as large as the man. The very pod that brought the man to Earth was decorated in his people's art. There were trees that used to stand centuries above him, bulls with grand horns, and a three eyed stone god. "I am Han Bullio!"

"Who?" Vayu asked.

"Bullio," Kataract yelled. "Rin!"

Bullio slammed his shield down so that it was facing the wind god. He planted his feet, and charged. Leaving a rut behind him, he crashed into Vayu with such force that it somehow stole the god's wind from his chest.

Kataract closed the gap behind the Baptized in Fire. He spun around the shield jabbed at the god, catching him between the third and fourth rib but not deep enough to do any immediate damage.

Vayu swung at Kataract with a wind gust but the Immortal ducked back behind the shield which didn't move against the combined might of the Eastreans.

"Rix," Kataract commanded.

Bullio tilted his shield forward so that Kataract had a chance to jump on the elephant man's shoulders. Kataract used the winds to guide him upward, then brought his sword down on Vayu. Vayu rolled out of the way then slid back to his feet in time to block Kataract's swings.

"Karura!" Vayu yelled. "Help me!"

Vayu looked around but saw no one. Just a lonely ship in need of a captain and crew. He sneered and turned back to his opponents just in time for Bullio to slam his shield into him again.

Vayu gasped and found words difficult, "I yield, let me go."

"Weakness?" Bullio complained. "Would you be so vulgar as to beg?"

"Go," Kataract said to the dissatisfaction of Bullio who stomped away. "I never wanted to fight in the first place."

"I suppose you might become accustomed to it," Vayu said. He whistled. A gazelle jumped next to him. Vayu climbed on top of it, nodded, and galloped away.

"Too easy," Bullio said. "You are too easy on him. Sark said you needed help and I came with haste. Then I don't get to settle it? I should have stayed by that pond with the others like me."

"I'm sorry, Bullio," Kataract said. "You can return to them if you wish."

"I do wish," Bullio said. He pounded his chest then saluted the Immortal. "And I shall manifest that wish in the hopes that I won't be disturbed by beings and their easily fixed problems."

Bullio trudged back down the mountain. He ranted about his hard work going in vain in hopes that the birds would be more understanding.

Kataract boarded The Reacher. He ran his fingers along the mast. He analyzed the grains in it and marveled at how intact it had remained. He would never tell anyone the ship's secret. He had managed to cut down a tree in Mangle's

Forest to reinforce the mast. The wood was easy to hack at once he broke away the bark. Most people focused on chopping which made the tree stronger. In that way, they were never able to make a dent.

"We've been through a lot," Kataract said to himself.

He took up the ropes and dropped the sails. He formed enough wind to bring him back up to the skies and drifted along in peace.

When he grew tired, he set The Reacher down in the ocean. He tightened the sails so that it held a steady course. He spun his fingers to guide the wind so that the seas weren't too harsh.

With the furnace below deck, Kataract cooked fish with a side of bowled eggs. He took up two plates and set them up at his table.

"Care to join me, Asha?" he said. "It's nothing like you are used to but it'll do."

The Karura emerged from behind a closed door. "You don't have to be so kind."

"Do you not breath?" Kataract said motioning for the plate. "You deserve more than kindness. Where would you like me to take you?"

"I don't want to go back," she said. She sat next him and pecked the food from her fingertips. She licked her beak and couldn't believe how good it was. Within a few moments, all that was left was a clean plate. "It was good."

"You can stay if you so wish it," Kataract said.

"Why would I?" Asha asked. "I am your enemy. A monster unfit for anyone's company."

"You are my equal," he countered. "And it is only an offer. I can take you anywhere."

She twisted her neck and noticed how lonely the living quarters felt. She wondered how he must have felt. If what Kataract had said was true, he must have been living in The Reacher longer than any god she knew had been alive.

"Then we shall be friends?" Asha asked. Her feathers ruffled in anticipation. She wasn't sure why, but she wanted to stay on the boat with the captain who controlled winds better than the gods.

Kataract smiled, "And what amazing friends we will be."

He stood and offered Asha his hand. She took it and shook, ready for their next adventure.

Colossals

Ration and Calypso were cloud watching in a field of poppies. The warm day was provided by the sun who was eager to meet with the moon in a few week's time. They rode in on the bulls, Baller and Baller, who accepted Calypso decorating them in flowers.

"So fierce you two are," Calypso told them. They seemed to nod in agreement. When she laughed, Ration felt his heart sink. "Look at you, my goddess. My love in her temple. Why don't you make a priest of this sinner?"

"I'm a titan, love," Calypso said, rolling her eyes. "Your silly words caught my heart already."

"Silly and true I suppose," Ration said.

The poppies began to swirl together. Their petals detached and came together to form a muscular man with dark features and long hair.

"Calypso look!" Atlas yelled. "Look at my lovely daughter!"

Calypso turned to him and the newborn baby in his arms. Ration ran over to him. The girl was wrapped in a blanket. Her black hair peaked out just enough to make the god want to twirl it.

"She's beautiful," Calypso said.

"Her name is Calypso," Atlas beamed. "I can think of no better name for two titans who are so loved."

Atlas raised the girl to the sky to show the sun. Clouds formed over the girl's face so to not blind her. The sun then peaked just enough over them to see.

"Are you sure?" Calypso asked. "That's not really how our naming works."

"Certainly!" Atlas said. "Do you have a problem with who I admire?"

"Of course not," Calypso stammered. "It's just, that I—"

"Ration!" Mal said, appearing from deep in the poppy field."

"Oh, thank the heavens," Calypso sighed.

"Trilo wants you," Mal continued.

"Gregorius!" Atlas said. "It's good to see you."

"Call me Mal, please," Mal said. "Only our families call us by our given name."

"That makes no sense but I will remember your wishes," Atlas said. "I apologize for this meeting being so short. Timing was never my best strength. Perhaps you all will join father and I for dinner?"

"We'd love to," Ration said. "Give Iapetus my regards."

Atlas walked off into the poppies. He kissed his daughter on the face and talked to her in a soft voice that he never afforded to show anyone else. The poppies lifted up again and swallowed him as they had spit him out.

Ration mounted Baller and offered his hand to Calypso.

"Are you sure?" She asked. "Trilo never cared for me."

"He'll have to figure out his own emotions. Besides he doesn't care about very many people." Ration reached down closer to her hand. She took it and was pulled up. "Care to take Baller, Mal?"

Mal gasped, "It, it would be an honor."

When Mal was situated and comfortable. Ration summoned a circle of flames. It engulfed them. Their skin turned to ash. Dust in the confines of creation, they found themselves dismantled and put together next to the god of stone.

"Pity you are so late," Trilo said with his arms crossed. "Your pup is as slow as ever."

"It's good to see you, my friend," Ration said with a smile. "Mal found me as fast as he could. He's limited compared to us so we shouldn't hold anything of the sort against him."

Mal whined but nodded in appreciation. He slipped off Baller but made sure the bull was between him and Trilo.

"You brought your pet, I see," The stone god said. Despite his fondness of the Titaness, Trilo always treated Calypso with hostility. He disapproved of everything about her and Ration's relationship. There were too many unknowns and too much that was left to be understood about these new gods.

"Still gaining frown marks under all your eyes I see,"

Calypso countered.

"Shouldn't you be making sure your king isn't eating children?" Trilo said.

"I don't meddle with the life of Cronus," Calypso said. "I don't have the strength to deal with him."

"He does," Trilo motioned to Ration who was scratching Baller and Baller on their foreheads. "He used to fix everything, you know. He could alter the flow of history at whim. Why doesn't he do it now. I wonder?"

"Fear, Trilo," Calypso explained. "He knows what that kind of control brings. The man has patience and appreciation for time. I adore that about him."

"Man? He is a god," Trilo said.

"That behaves like a man," Calypso studied Ration as he tried to motion for Mal to come out in the open and join them. "Neither of us will ever understand him. It's not in our essence. We can learn from him though. Beg, pray even, to be better. Sometimes it takes lose reins to guide the horse and I think we can grow to understand that."

"Trilo," Ration interrupted. "You wanted to show me something."

"Something better than you have ever done," Trilo corrected.

Trilo snapped his fingers. From all around them, the Earth shook. From its surface came people that blocked out the sun with their grotesque size. They were dressed in the earth itself but held no emotion to the deities below them.

"People?" Ration said. His expression was that of concern, not amazement as Trilo had hoped.

"Giant ones!" Trilo grinned. "Much better than anything you could create."

"I have some concerns," Ration said.

"Of course you do," Trilo complained. "What are they?"

"What if they decide to be conquerors as humans are showing to be," Ration asked. He strained his neck to find the tops of the new race of man.

"They won't," Trilo said. "I will control them so that it isn't possible. They will build an empire like no other has seen."

"What about their free will?" Ration asked.

"They won't have any," Trilo expressed. "They will do exactly as I say."

"Then what's the point?" Ration asked.

"That they are great!" Trilo said.

"They are, I assure you," Ration said. "But your goal is to be better than me, correct? How are they better if they aren't naturally that way? Honestly, my friend, I don't see them lasting more than a thousand years."

"I bet you they last longer than the people of this world," Trilo said.

"What would you stake on it?" Ration said. "I would give you my knowledge if it meant you would trust me."

"My middle eye," Trilo said.

"You would give up your sight over the planet?" Ration asked.

"I haven't been able to see since we arrived. Why should I keep it?" Trilo glared down on Ration.

"Fine," Ration agreed. "Only if you give them free will."

Trilo snapped his fingers. The giants fell to the ground. They tried to stand but found it difficult under their weight.

One started to chew on a boulder. Another gazed up at the sky and tried to catch a cloud.

"Give them time," Ration said. "My people had millions of years to progress and learn. The rushed will find their flaws quicker."

Mal was a little less worried about Trilo but maintained his distance. He decided to stay by the gods side and offer support.

Ration mounted Baller and Calypso joined him. He took the other Baller by the reins and tied him to the saddle.

"I can't wait to see how amazing they are, Trilo," Calypso called as they trotted off through another portal of fire and back to their home.

"Did you know that was going to happen to them?" she asked Ration.

"In a way," he said as he set her off the bull. "Pyre told me. It was like I saw it in a memory."

"Memories don't happen in the future," Calypso pointed out.

"I know," Ration said.

She raised an eyebrow but he didn't say anything further on the idea.

"I worry about him," Ration said to change the subject back. "He's always been distant and direct. Change hurts him in a way. I think he doesn't want something like Eastrea to happen again. I think I need some time to think."

"Of course," Calypso said. "Take your time."

"Thank you." He kissed her for a half second longer than normal. He then handed the bulls over to be put away and walked through the fields.

When he was far enough away, Ration allowed himself

a sigh of release.

"You know this will all eventually be destroyed," Pyre said in Ration's head.

"Believe what you think," Ration said.

"It is in our nature to destroy," Pyre said.

"And create," Ration said.

"Destroy everything, then create again," Pyre said.

"Even Calypso?" Ration asked.

"Except Calypso," Pyre said. "There are few perfections in the universe and they shouldn't be meddled with."

"What about Lanta, or Wallace, or Louse?" Ration asked.

"I do not wish them harm, they are friends," Pyre said.

"And Trilo?" Ration asked.

"Though I wish it, he is a necessity for now," Pyre said.

"See, you are not all doom and gloom," Ration laughed.

"Destruction is a necessity, Ration," Pyre explained. "It must happen to create an appreciation for this world."

Ration picked up a hand full of grass. He studied their intricate designs. The way their cells and atoms came together to form the essence of their existence.

"Do you not think we wouldn't love this world if it lasted," Ration asked Pyre.

"Permanence has no value, fire god. All those who survived know this."

"Yet I made it so they could have permanence," Ration said.

"Could have, not will have," Pyre corrected. "Your

compassion will cause others pain."

"Or set them at ease," Ration tried. "I might surprise you."

"How many of your lifetimes do you think I've consumed?"

"You would be the one to know, Pyre," Ration said.

"Billions," Pyre urged. "I have seen Ration's come and go and time will always start again. It is by my decree. As much as you try to split my power it is *my* will. Time starts with Eastrea and ends with Earth. Look to the sky. You saw Trilo's giants. You saw how they towered far beyond what you thought was possible. How much of that sky do you think I can take over now?"

Ration held up his hand and covered a portion of the sky. "About that much."

"*All* of it and farther," Pyre explained.

"Only?"

"I am infinite everything and infinite nothing, Ration. You are my vessel and are just as important as I am. You only give me time to become the universe once again. I have predicted everything that has happened and will happen." Pyre seemed to rumble in a sort of longing that could only be calmed by death.

"Yet you were surprised by Louse," Ration said.

"Parts of a second for me," Pyre said.

"Just enough for hope," Ration said.

"I suppose I am also surprised by your never-ending optimism," Pyre grumbled.

"What comes of Trilo's giants?" Ration asked.

"They become a part of the history of the world. Barrick and Arsenal will know," Pyre fell quiet in Ration.

"Always good listening to you, Pyre," Ration said.

He looked at the clouds that drifted over the fields. He took a hand and covered the same portion of the sky that he did before. He then took his other hand and made it so that none of the sky was visible.

"I think I'll have to surprise you, god of destruction and creation," he said out loud.

* * * * *

Graphite woke from his mid-day nap at the same moment Trilo woke his giants.

He traced the ground. With the tips of his fingers, he made a track in the dirt like a snake on its way to its den. The way the earth shook with their arrival made him remember his debut as a god.

An Icarian with cat like features ran into the cavern. It bowed low and said, "Forgive me, my lord."

"What is it?" Graphite asked the creature.

"Our forces have gathered," It explained. "We need only you to command us. What would you have us do?"

"I have yet to decide," Graphite said. "You will be reformed into my vision. I will not be the god you wish me to be. I am Eastrean before your puppet."

The Icarian bowed lower. "Yes, my lord."

Graphite exited his cave. Icarians flooded the valley, ready for their god's orders. They cheered when they saw him. Clashing shields, the roar of the new Icarian army made the god bow back.

The Water God

Lanta rode atop Wallace's horns as he pushed through the deep snow. She was too small to make any distance. Wallace, on the other hand, was able to guide them up the ancient Himalayan mountain with ease.

"I heard one of the grave diggers are up here, Nathanial," Lanta said.

"I don't pay too much attention to rumors, Ida," Wallace said. "Though it wouldn't surprise me. They have a sense for where they're needed."

Usually, an Eastrean was only referred to by their family or region they hailed from. In those smaller communities they would then be called by their first name. Tristan, Kataract, and Carca were exceptions to this rule as they were typically seen as outcasts and were associated with their trade skills and not their place of orient.

"Are they needed?" Lanta asked.

"Depends on Sepron's mood," Wallace panted. He was becoming increasingly frustrated with the magnitude of the snow. Their armor's weight made them down so they sunk lower than a mortal would and despite his abnormal strength, made the journey harsh. "I thought Eastrea had bad storms."

"You're doing great, Nathanial," Lanta encourage.

"Thank you, really," Wallace said. Lanta rubbed her feet on his shoulders for extra effect.

"I think the snow was heavier on Eastrea," Lanta reminisced. "It was dangerous if you were caught in the open because of how much it tore away at you. Here, it's light, but sticky. Almost like it wants to suffocate you. A cute attempt to be sure."

Wallace laughed and dug deeper. With each motion, he could feel himself getting closer to the water god.

Ration had told the two he had lost contact with Sepron and was beginning to worry. He knew he was alive but nothing much after that. With little more than a gut feeling, they had left the Mediterranean and were headed to the peak of the world.

Wallace and Lanta had trekked to just a few miles from the top before breaking for camp. With just two shields, it was small but comfortable. The shields provided warmth when needed so there was no need to build a fire that would dwindle at their strength.

To pass the time, they traded stories as they usually did. The years that had brought them together made the stories repetitive, but they enjoyed the company of their closest friend.

The next morning, a tall, hairy, white beast met them.

He scratched his chest and offered the two a goat he captured, to which they shook their heads.

"MY MOUNTAIN WILL FOREVER BE YOUR HOME, CHILDREN OF PYRE," the ape man said.

"We were talking about you yesterday Etchet," Wallace greeted. "It's good to see you."

Etchet buried his face in his goat. With a split and a smack of his lips, he said, "SEPRON HAS BEEN HERE FOR TOO LONG. THE SNOWS WILL BE HERE LONGER THAN ANYONE COULD DREAM. THE GOD OF WATER WILL LEAVE HIS IMPACT TO BE SURE."

"We'll talk to him," Wallace said. He eyed the goat in between Etchet's fingers. He tried to think of other things other than the possibility of it being a ram. "Would you care to join us?"

"AS LONG AS MY MEAL IS WELCOME, I WILL JOIN," Etchet said.

"Of course!" Lanta said. "It'll be good to find what you have been doing for all these years."

They started to walk to where they believed Sepron was with Etchet parting the newly fallen snow ahead of them.

"I HAVE BEEN SEARCHING," he said. "MY HEAD TELLS ME THERE WILL BE SOULS LOST HERE. SOULS WITH AMBITION AND IGNORANCE. THEY WILL FIND THIS MOUNTAIN AND SEE THE CHALLENGE THAT IT POSSESSES. THEN I WILL GUIDE THEM ONWARD TO THEIR AFTERLIFE AS DEATH HAS COMMANDED ME AND ALL GRAVEDIGGERS TO DO WITH LOST SOULS."

"Blazes, Etchet," Wallace said. "Do you know any jokes?"

"NO," the beast said. "ONLY POETRY…

"FOR HERE I AM,
LOST IN A WORLD SO LONELY.
MY SOUL WILL ONLY KNOW THOSE WHO CAN NOT STAY LONG.
LOST IN A WORLD WHERE MY OWN SOUL CAN NOT KNOW THE SAME KINDNESS.

"THAT IS ALL."

"Beautiful?" Lanta said. She tilted her head at Wallace.

"THANK YOU, DAUGHTER OF EASTREA," Etchet said.

"What has the night moon been doing?" Wallace said, eager to change the subject.

"HE HAS DONE AS HE ALWAYS DONE," Etchet explained. "HE FINDS THOSE THAT ARE WEARY. THOSE THAT FIND THEMSELVES LOST IN THE COUNTLESS INFINITY THAT DEATH ALLOWS ALL TO EXPERIENCE."

Lanta let out a deep breath and widened her eyes.

"I THINK I WILL MAKE MY HOME HERE. THE COLD FEELS GOOD UPON MY SKIN. MY FUR WILL HELP ME STAY HIDDEN AMONGST THE SNOW. MY TIME MAY BE TOO EARLY, PERHAPS, BUT I WILL BE PATIENT. THOSE ADVENTURERS ARE SURE TO COME. BLIZZARDS HIDE THOSE LOST IN ITS BLANKET OF HOPELESSNESS. I HEAR THEM CALL. I HEAR THEM WAIL IN THEIR DEATH. FEAR GRIPS THEM WHEN THEY SEE ME. I ESCORT THEM JUST THE SAME. I BURY THEIR BODIES TO THE BEST OF MY ABILITY. I HOPE THEY REST WELL IN THEIR AFTERLIFE. HERE IS OUR GOD."

The last line made the Baptized shake their heads.

Etchet's words, though cumbersome, lulled them into a sort of slumber that made them forget they were following the Gravedigger. They rubbed their eyes, yawned, and stretched.

Sepron stood over the world. His arms were outstretched as if ready to embrace all those who did not know his name.

"Look at them all," Sepron said. "Not a single soul knows of us. Do you know that?"

"Maybe we should check in with people more," Lanta said.

"Hush, Ida," Wallace chastised.

"Is it possible for a god to lose faith in another?" Sepron asked. He turned to the other Eastreans. "Ration knows more than he will tell. I feel like this world is familiar. However, how can I know a world I have never been to. Do you know the feeling?"

They exchanged looks. They all knew that the universe was cyclical. They knew that within time Eastrea would rise again but their current selves wouldn't be there. All Eastreans went to the Interworlds where their previous souls rested.

"Pyre is the only one who knows what is going to happen," Wallace offered. "We, as Eastreans, all know this."

"I've been watching. There are holes in my vision. One for Ration and Pyre as they conspire with other gods. Trilo blocks me at every opportunity. Then there is one more that grows. It feels Eastrean in nature, yet all Eastrean's are accounted for. Who could it be? If Pyre knows all, why hasn't he told anyone what it is? Why is it so familiar to me, yet not threatening?"

"If it isn't threatening, why should you care?" Wallace asked.

"Because the veil around Trilo and Ration feel threatening to me. Nearly every entity in this world feels like it wants us gone. I can *feel* it in the droplets in every part of the world. They tell me to prepare. To be ready to draw them near. Why do I hear my past selves warn me?"

"You can hear the Interworlds?" Lanta asked.

"Can you not?" Sepron said. "We might be powerful but death is always a short swim away. All it takes is for someone patient enough to pull us under."

"Nathanial, maybe we should go," Lanta said.

Wallace was watching Etchet who had set down his goat. The giant's hair was standing on end as he listened to the Sepron talk.

"DEATH SURROUNDS YOU, MY GOD," he said.

"Is that a threat, Gravedigger?" Sepron asked.

"AN OBSERVATION," Etchet said.

Lanta tapped Wallace's horns, "Nathanial, please. We know where he is and that he's safe. I'm getting uncomfortable."

"Me too," he whispered to her. He turned to Sepron and said, "It's good to see you God of Water. We were ordered to seek you out and to make sure you were safe. That is done and we must be going now."

"Do as you must," Sepron said.

Wallace pivoted away. He held his shield close to him so that it covered his other hand on his crossbow. Lanta turned around in her seat to watch Etchet and Sepron. They didn't follow them. they didn't even watch them. Sepron faced the world again with his arms outstretched.

"They're on edge," Lanta said to Wallace.

"We should be too," he said.

"We'll stick together for what they see, right?" Lanta asked.

"I don't think I know any other way," Wallace said. He allowed himself to release his crossbow. He then placed a hand on Lanta's back. She didn't allow herself the luxury to relax until after the two beings were out of sight.

Monsters in Man

Trilo **coughed into his** arm. His stone eyes were shallow. A tinge of blue peaked out from behind the caverns that were his sockets.

"You're not looking too well, my friend," Ration noted. "Is there anything I should know about."

Trilo shot him a wicked glance but it eased just as quick. "I'm not sure. I've been feeling drained in this world. I feel as though my power is no longer of stone and my purpose cannot be fulfilled."

"I'll take some time to think on it," Ration noted.

Tal Alex flicked her tongue. "The air around you taste different. You're still just as powerful but it is as if your essence it not... present."

Kanter Flass ruffle her feathers and murmured, "She's lucky he isn't in his usual mood."

"Thank you," Trilo said. "I do not know of your nature

but some enlightenment is appreciated."

The other Eastreans exchanged looks. This was the first time any of them had heard the god be grateful.

"Maybe you should pass on this one," Ration suggested.

"I must maintain at least the vision of power," Trilo said. "Though I ask none of you mention this process. Whatever it may be."

They all nodded in agreement.

"The veil we've sensed has covered a great area," Ration said.

"And the center moves as we do," Trilo added.

"Are you suggesting your worries are Eastrean in origin?" Flass said. "How would that be possible?"

"It's possible," Alex added. "Eastrea crumbled. We saw it. Well Wallace was the one to see. Maybe a piece fell later."

Flass nodded, "There were a lot of asteroids there for a while."

"We didn't move that often," Alex said. "We were negligent."

"Did we have any reason to not be?" Flass asked.

"Not until those first gods," Alex said. "Then we were divided as our interests grew."

"Divided and conquered?" Flass asked.

"If we were at full strength," Alex said.

"We haven't measured our strength yet," Flass said.

"There's too many unknowns at the moment," Alex said. "I'll have to make an assessment. If that is fine with you, my lord."

"I don't see why not," Ration said.

"I do," Pyre said.

"Hush," Ration said out loud. When he noticed that the others were looking at him, the fire god gave a shy smile, "Sorry, I was in my own head for a moment."

"You're fine," Alex said. "However, it would be nice to know that our gods can protect us."

"We'll do our best," Ration said.

"That's not reassuring," Flass said. "Thank you."

Ration laughed.

Their journey brought them to the mouth of a cave where the tree had all abandoned any effort for growth and only the rodents of the world danced among the rocky surface.

"I can taste something odd in there," Alex said. She tightened the strap on her shield. Flass followed suit. She drew her crossbow and stepped behind Alex.

Alex planted her shield into the ground, then tilted it just enough to give them cover while also being short enough for the other Baptized to have a clear shot at anything that came for them.

"I've always admired your choice in people," Trilo said. "The pure instinct they seemed to have out shone anything I could create."

"Your people shook all of Eastrea," Ration said. "Equals in their own right."

"How should we proceed?" Flass asked. The feathers on her wings fluttered with anticipation.

"Wait out here and join us if you see anyone," Ration said.

"We should consider this as hostile territory," Trilo added.

"Acknowledged," the Baptized said together.

They shifted their shields to sit long ways against the ground. They sat shoulder to shoulder in opposite directions. Both of their crossbows were out now. Flass guarded the cavern and Alex scanned the valley below.

"After you," Trilo said.

Ration entered with a familiar feeling warning him.

The stalactites dripped at a steady rate, echoing their slow voices to the gods.

Trilo closed his eyes into a smile, "That sound is endearing. It's progress through patience. Not that you would see life in a rock."

"I don't just hear Pyre, Trilo," Ration said. He held out a hand and caught a drop. It instantly evaporated against his skin. "I hear every molecule, every atom breaking down and coming together. Besides perhaps Sepron and Barrick, I might be the only one that understands just what you are talking about."

"This is the first time we've talked about our powers," Trilo said.

"I never see you, friend," Ration said. "We haven't had the chance to talk about anything other than my faults."

"I might need to change that," Trilo said.

A stalagmite broke and crashed to the floor. Ration wheeled around, started a small flame in his hand, and prepared himself to throw. Trilo, who sensed the being and felt unthreatened, only watched farther down the cave.

A hooded man with white hair stood tall against his own shadow. Lightning danced from his fingertips, making small pops as they fizzled out.

"Can we help you?" Ration asked.

"Leave the god be, Ration," Trilo urged. "He's not the

one casting the veil."

"You two saw it too?" The god said.

"Yes, now go away," Trilo said. He trudged further down the cave.

"I apologize for him," Ration said. "I am Ration, the Eastrean god of Fire, he is Trilo, the god of stone. Who are you if I might ask?"

The god thought for a moment. He had no idea where Eastrea was. He had traveled the world in an attempt to hide from his father. The same father whose power seemed to radiate in a separate part of this new god. Despite his instincts telling him otherwise, he said, "I am Zeus. I'm afraid I'm not a god of anything. Yet. There's a prophecy that says—"

"A young god exploring forces he can't even wish to understand," Trilo interrupted. "What a joy."

"I'll have you know that fate favors me!" Zeus said. "Besides, how would a god with so little followers and prayers know about forces of the world?"

"Fate?" Trilo laughed. "Fate is tied to that meek god next to you. We are above those silly prayers of yours. We do not need stories to fuel our essence."

"Is that so?" Zeus said. "What is your story?"

"Must you follow us?" Trilo pleaded.

"I created the universe," Ration said in attempt to deflect Trilo's hostility. "Well, Pyre did, the creation and destruction god inside me. When the time comes, we destroy it, though I don't know how. He won't tell me. With each cycle, time goes on further and further. I can only imagine how many of you have existed."

Ration laughed at the thought but Zeus did not.

"Then what is your opinion on how I am fated to

rule?" Zeus asked. "If the fire god willed the information."

"He won't tell you," Trilo said. "He will only say what he's allowed to say from those books of his past."

"Books?" Zeus asked.

"You'll see eventually," Ration said.

"Are you two normally this cryptic?" Zeus asked.

"Only on our good days," Trilo said. "You don't want to see how direct we are on our bad ones."

"Trilo," Ration urged. "Quit being so rude to the young god. He'll have to find his own way."

"GET OUT OF MY HEAD!" a scream called from just in front of the gods. "I need you, please… GET OUT OF MY HEAD!"

A ghostly hand gripped a stalagmite. Its claws started to scrape it before black chains pulled the hand to the monster's head. It tried to reach at them with the other hand but the same chains held it to its heart.

"Please, show kindness," it said.

* * * * *

"Why us?" Alex asked Flass.

"Why indeed," Flass replied. She grinded her beak. "There were others who could have been paired with Trilo."

"I don't blame Wallace and Lanta," Alex said. "Or Bullio. Mal and Warftuff have had a better time getting along with him. They should have come."

"Warftuff hasn't been themselves lately," Flass explained. "After War God's army fell, they felt as though their leadership wasn't the most qualified. Nobody has been able to find them."

"I didn't realize," Alex said. "I've been a little removed. Things have changed so fast."

"For us," Flass said. "To the world, it has been an eternity since we've arrived. If Arsenal hadn't slowed down time for us, the next cycle would feel like tomorrow."

"The air..." Alex said. She flicked her tongue. "It can't be."

A guttural howl came from the forest just below the cave. Then outstepped a wolf headed beast in plated armor. He raised a rusted sword at the Baptized. His gaze met them as they stared back in disbelief.

As he lowered his sword, he snapped a command which unleashed dozens of the thought to be extinct Icarians.

* * * * *

"What is that thing?" Trilo asked. He wrinkled his nose and took a step back. He turned his head to the faint sound of metal clashing and beasts roaring outside. He knew the Baptized could handle whatever was attacking.

"A monster," Zeus said.

"A human," Ration said. "Lost to his mind."

"How can you call it so?" Zeus asked. "Look at it. That is not the face or body of a human."

"But his hands and eyes and voice are," Ration explained. He reached out to the monster. "His mind has Lost its humanity, but not those things."

The monster recoiled away from the gods. "No. no. NO!" it muttered over and over again. Its eyes flashed around the cave. They begged for a familiar presence but ignored the gods.

"We should kill it," Zeus said. Sparks started to snap around his finger tips until a lightning bolt flashed into his hands. The bolts arched between his palms to do just that until Ration caught him. The lightning faded and snapped into nothing again.

"You just took my power?" Zeus complained. "Why shouldn't we kill it? Does something so horrible really deserve an existence in this world."

"You're thinking about Sark," Trilo said. "The mute didn't deserve your patience either."

"I will *always* firmly disagree." Ration stared into Zeus's eyes. They both challenged each other in unwavering pride that wouldn't allow either to resign their decision.

* * * * *

Flass flew up with a cat-like Icarian's shoulders in her talons. Alex wrapped around its legs and together they ripped it in half from the ribs down. They let it fly across the attacking members of the long-forgotten troop which did nothing to slow the attack.

As Flass landed, she unslung her crossbow. She let out a volley of bolts that flattened a row of roaring Icarians.

"I thought they were dead!" she yelled.

"Better go back to thought," Alex said. She swiped up with her sword, catching a wolf-like Icarian under its jaw and exited out the top of its skull. It side stepped and spun around just in time for Flass to drive her sword into its chest. It fell gurgling on its own blood.

A bear-like Icarian extended its claws for Alex. She swung her sword around but it jumped back. It slammed its paws on the ground but before it could attack it fell silent. Its ears twinged then retreated back away from the Baptized.

The other Icarians followed suit. Lining the hillside, they all bowed their heads then split into two groups with a walkway that lead into the forest.

The ground shook and rumbled. In the blink of an eye, it opened up around Flass and Alex. Boulders sprung out to trap them in such a way that they couldn't move their arms or legs. Only their hands and heads stuck out from the rock.

"What's going on? Trilo?" Alex struggled to say. She cranked her head around to see if he was coming out of the cave but there was no one.

"Alex," Flass said. "The trees. It came from the trees."

A man stepped out from the clearing. His brown armor was the same as the last day they saw him talking to their god, Ration. With every step, their hearts began to race faster. Their eyes never left the old general. Wide with anticipation.

When he reached to the two Baptized, he raised his hand. They both flinched away, waiting for the strike. Instead, he patted Alex's head.

"You'll be safe," the man said. "This has been long overdue."

He entered the cave.

"Ration!" Flass yelled. "Graphite! Graphite is here! Ration!"

* * * * *

Ration had explained Max Sark's story. From their enlistment to their transformation into an Icarian and back to an Eastrean.

Zeus wrinkled his nose. "Such a disgusting thing. You should abandon the fool."

"I believe I made my stance clear," Ration said. He crossed his arms. In his peripheral-right, he saw the monster crawling through the stalagmites. It muttered to itself as one hand clawed at its face and the other reached for the gods.

"I've seen you in my wonderings," Zeus said. "You live in my lands but you are not from them. What says your way is better than mine."

Chills ran under Ration's skin. The way the other god said he had *seen* him. Like he knew exactly who Ration was. Who he was aligned with. Who he called friends and family.

"I seek understanding," Ration said at last. "Maybe I can work to eliminate this sort of creation. These monsters that form from man."

"It is in their nature to be able to form monsters," Zeus explained. "Although there are those amongst the gods that act just as beastly. A certain king of the Titans comes to mind."

"Cronus is who I assume you are talking about," Ration noted. "His actions are not my own and it is not my place to intervein in his *particular* diet. Most of the Titans only follow out of fear."

"And are you afraid?" Zeus said.

Ration said nothing. He only stared into Zeus's eyes. Sparks collided inside them as they threatened the embers in Rations.

"I have the feeling you know what I'm afraid of," Ration said. He forced the image of Calypso and the Eastreans out of his mind. He had no idea what the extent of this god's abilities were. Protecting himself against any possible threats would be a priority.

He took a deep breath to clear his mind. Immediately, he sensed what he had was sure of so long ago.

A face that should have been forgotten several million years before slowly made itself visible.

"Ration, Trilo," Graphite said. "I thought it might be you I sensed down here."

"Graphite?" Trilo said. He brought forward his hammer but felt his strength wane from his arms. "You're supposed to be dead!"

Sparks of electricity launched from Zeus's finger tips and into a column of stone that sprung from the ground to protect the Icarian god.

"That's my power!" Trilo boomed. "You've stolen it from me!"

"It wasn't my intention, I assure you." Graphite rubbed his eyes then squinted in the dark. "There you are, sir."

Graphite walked past the gods. First Zeus who eyed these gods that seemed to deflect his every effort to establish himself, then Ration who wouldn't meet his gaze, then Trilo who scowled at him as he tried to lift his hammer.

The creature huddled behind his stone. When it looked up at Graphite, it stopped it's rambling. To it, Graphite appeared as a light of warmth. When he touched its face, the warmth transferred into its body. Encasing the monster is a dull glow, the next thing the gods saw was a new being.

Instead of the shriveled heap that they pitied, there was a fully formed Icarian with bear like features. It looked at its hands. Then spoke in Icarian to the new stone god.

"Go, there will be others waiting for you outside," Graphite said. "Ignore the two covered in stone."

"You've been healing them," Ration said. "Every time

I found a disturbance, it was gone long before I could get there."

"He's creating an army," Trilo said. "We should end this here."

"I think this is a matter for Eastreans," Ration said. He motioned for Zeus to leave.

Zeus grit his teeth. How dare these foreign gods make a mockery of him. They barely acknowledged his power and now dismissed him without a care for him.

"I disagree," Zeus argued.

"Leave," Ration urged. He shot the god a glance that knocked Zeus off his feet. *So cold. Such power.* He scrambled to regain his composure, then, with a boom disappeared in a shroud of lightning.

"What are you planning?" Ration asked.

"Nothing," Graphite said. "This world has been abandoning people. I bring them their sanity in the only way I can. They are more than welcome to leave us after some education."

"Which is?" Trilo asked. He sheathed his hammer behind his back. He didn't lower his guard, however. If there was a fight, it would have to be Ration who finished it.

"We explain how the world sees them," Graphite said. He didn't acknowledge Trilo in his answer. He spoke as if he was going to explain anyways and pretended that the former stone god wasn't there. "There are all manner of monsters that plague these lands. Humanity has varying views on them. Mostly hostile. I do not want my position. However, I am stuck in it. I might as well do the best I can for the people that entrust their support in me."

"Which just so happens to be *the* largest threat that we

have yet to face," Trilo said.

"Are you a threat now?" Ration asked.

"Only if we need to be," Graphite replied.

"Do you need to be?" Trilo asked.

"We should have an arrangement," Ration said.

Graphite scowled at Ration. He could tell anything he had to say would be dismissed, no matter how he loud he made sure he was heard. Besides, he didn't have the strength to defend his words.

"If our interests do not align, there will be conflict," Ration said.

"We will not seek it," Graphite said. "Though we have just as much right to defend ourselves."

"Understandable," Ration agreed.

"You two should know," Graphite started. He glanced over to make sure Trilo was paying attention. "A group split from us. They made me their god to enforce their old ways. When I changed the direction of Icarian interest, they were less than pleased. If you come across them, I recommend extreme caution. From my understanding they are still in search of a god to represent them."

"Thank you," Ration said.

"Of course," Graphite said. "And Ration… When Eastrea fell, I saw Pyre's plan. On accident or purpose, I cannot say. Do you know it?"

"I do," Ration nodded. "I've always known."

"Are you going to do anything about it?" Graphite asked. "*Is* there anything to do about it?"

"I don't know," Ration said.

Part 2

Gods of the Flood

Gods of Dust

"**Are we going to** honor that?" Sark asked.

Ration and Trilo had just finished explaining their encounter with Graphite to the participating Eastreans. The only ones who were not in attendance were Sepron, Carca, Louse, and Arsenal. The Gravediggers were present as well, though they had made it clear they didn't think they should be included. Non-Eastreans included Calypso and Neith, who sat next to their husbands, and the small yet loyal crew of Kataract. Calypso had her hands resting on her stomach which stuck out through her robes.

"We should," Ration said. "This is our home now and we knew what conflict with Icarians can lead to."

"And what about this other group?" Barrick asked. "Should we hunt them down?"

"From our understanding they are in a completely different region of the world," Ration said. He scratched his face as he stared away from his group. "I don't think they will be a problem for a long time. Humanity hasn't migrated there yet so their numbers must be the same. Near as I can see they aren't an immediate threat."

"And the immediate threat is what?" Kataract asked.

"How do you mean?" Ration asked.

"We are spread all across the world," The Immortal of Currents explained. "And none of them like us. They tolerate us. We've been seeing more and more hostility. War god was small scale. We handled him. This says more to me."

Barrick nodded. "We should prepare. Set has been less than pleased about our marriage and there are whispers of rebellion. And this Zeus you mentioned has an air of destiny about him. Louse described him in one of her visions."

"Did she now?" Ration said. "I won't hear any more of her visions if it's all the same. If you want your future known—"

"I don't," Barrick said. "I stopped her before she went too far. She is worried about something. Though she babbles I think we should hear her out. At least make sense of her prophecies."

"No," Ration commanded. "Let time unfold onto us. Knowing our fates won't change them. I hear you all. Go, and if anything in the world arises, let me know as soon as possible. We will resolve it then."

The Eastreans went to their newfound homes with the wave of a hand. The only ones who remained were Barrick and the wives. Neith rested her hand on Barrick's shoulder.

"Is there anything we can do? Maybe Ra can raise a force."

"If he can spare it," Ration said. "Thank you."

"Can Cronus spare anything?" Neith asked.

"He isn't the giving sort," Calypso explained. "His hand is tight on his kingdom and with our marriage we agreed to not take part in any Titan affairs. Unfortunately, we're on our own on our end of the world."

"We were invited to the summit tomorrow, my love," Ration said. He scratched the ends of both his elbows. He looked to the sky as he wondered on his luck. "Perhaps then we can entertain the idea in his head. "

Calypso shook her head. "That is a big perhaps. The prophecy has filled him with paranoia."

"Lots of talk about prophecy these days," Neith said. "It might be best to hear Louse out. After all, an idea of what is to come might help us prepare."

"I stand by my husband on this matter," Calypso said. "These things have a way of coming to pass no matter how precautions are made."

Neith frowned at the titaness. She bit her lip at the thought, then shot a glance at her beloved. At their wedding, Louse had given her a prophecy which now range in the back of her mind:

Barrick will bring change to the times of gods.
Be feared and loved with Friend's guidance.
You will watch him though he does not know it.
I see only tears of the thought of your going.

* * * * *

1 week later

Arsenal stretched his ball of yarn. In it, he saw himself walking through the deserts of early Israel. "Well, we're still headed in the right direction. Are you sure Louse didn't give a reason for being here? It might help us track her sooner."

Carca nodded. She kicked some sand at Arsenal's shadow. It realized it was late again and rushed under its owner. "She said she wanted to learn from different oracles. To try to figure out how to control her foresight. Why here I can't tell. The earth is getting easier to translate but near as I can tell there are only a few gods here that specialize in planning and prophecy."

"And?"

Carca sighed. "That's as much as the world wants to tell me. I think it knows were aren't supposed to be here. It keeps calling me this word I haven't figured out yet. I think it's like foreigner but there is a hostility in it. Parasite maybe. I don't know. I've been distracted lately."

"I know," Arsenal reassured. He wrapped her in a side hug. She turned her face to the ground. "You're doing great. Maybe talking about it will help."

"I appreciate your friendship," Carca said. "I just don't understand Ration. He made rules that he is somehow free from. I mean, Trilo and Sepron have to follow the rules. Barrick even reinforced some of them. Why is Ration the only one to act on his own?"

She brushed away from Arsenal and started to walk along their same path. Arsenal looked over the edge of the cliffs they were standing on. A river had cut its path long before they had gotten there. Grasses grew along the riverbed where various animals took opportunities from the plentiful resources that flocked there.

Arsenal saw people carving into the cliff side just underneath him. They hadn't noticed them so he watched them as he thought on Carca's words.

"I think as a host of Pyre, he is allowed certain privileges," Arsenal said as he caught up to Carca.

She ruffled her wings at the sound of the creation god. "Right. Our other deity. I hear the world talk about him a lot."

"I don't think we talk about him enough," Arsenal said. He made sure to meet her eyes. "You told me that Ration loses control sometimes. Do we need to worry?"

"You tell me," she said. For the first time since their journey Carca met Arsenal's gaze. "You hold the strings of time in your fingertips. You can see every possible outcome at once. What do you make of our future?"

"It doesn't work like that," Arsenal admitted. He found himself being ashamed. Ashamed that he hadn't yet found out every detail of how his immortality worked. Ashamed that he couldn't do any more to set the other Eastrean's minds at ease. He knew he was just a conduit to keep time on course and yet everything he desired to know seemed to be just out of reach. "I can only see my future and only as far as my fingers allow. I have to squeeze the yarn at our current place and even then, I see only a few moments ahead. I also have to have been there in my past self to see it. Time is memory and I can't see what I haven't remembered. It is only by luck or rather necessity in the past that I can see our current path. This is the first that you are here with me. That makes things a little more difficult but not too much so."

"Why wasn't I with you before?" Carca asked.

"Near as I can tell, you stayed with the Titans and Ration. Although, I'm happy to have the company." Arsenal nudged Carca and gave her a large smile. "Keep your head up. Things will get better. It will get easier."

… "You've seen it?"

"Things have to better eventually. The only way for things to remain bad is if we stay in that place. It's not in our nature to stay miserable forever."

Carca smiled up at Arsenal. "Thank you for being a good friend. That means a lot."

Arsenal pulled out his yarn. He traced his fingers to find where they were currently. In it, he saw himself walking up to Louse and another being next to her. His alabaster wings shrouded her. He whispered to her and spoke with his hands. Eyes of a thousand colors circled around him.

"Be ready," he said. Carca's wings tightened. "We found her but there's someone with her."

It was the deity that noticed them first though Louse turned to them just after him.

"Arsenal?" She said. She shot up from her seat. "Carca? What brings you here?"

"We're checking up on you," Carca said. "Ration held a meeting and no one heard your response."

"Oh, I knew what it was about," Louse said. Her face was covered by a woolen shawl. It was tied tight around her nose and mouth leaving her chin exposed. Her eyes showed a smile that was trying not to laugh. "I tried to tell Ration but he wouldn't have it. Now, I'm just wondering. This world is so beautiful. I never had a chance to explore Eastrea but I remember it's harshness."

She turned her head to the sky. "Even the clouds and stars have meaning here. Isn't it amazing?"

Carca looked up but she couldn't tell any more about the formless clouds than she had in the past. "It's going to rain this evening."

"The stars tell these peoples stories," Arsenal said. "They are formed by them. Barrick loves to fill my ears with them. Maybe you should talk with him soon."

"I'd love that," Louse smiled. "First, I would like to finish my conversation with Michael."

The deity waved. "We were talking about futures. We only have prophecies that have been told to us by God. It is my duty to follow through."

"Follow through as what?" Carca said. She flapped her wings in recognition of their similar trait.

Michael mimicked her motion, "As an angel. I have a lot to be expected of me in the future, you see. What are you two? Louse told me of her nose but I had no idea others with wings and a being with such interesting eyes existed. I suppose I should try to explore more."

Arsenal materialized an apple. He offered it to the angel. Before Michael could take it, it vaporized. Arsenal sighed, "So that's where I pulled it from."

Michael's head snapped to the side then the brightness in his face faded. "I accept your disappearing fruit as an offering. Still, I can pretend to know the taste. Mm. Akin to air."

"I am Arsenal Umber, the Immortal of Time," Arsenal explained. "And Carca, the Immortal of Medicines. We were created with these attributes though I suppose my eyes were intended to help me see the timeline of this world."

"I've wondered their intent myself," Carca said. "They don't function like one of our Baptized—"

"Baptized?" Michael noted. "We might be closer to understanding each other than we realize."

Carca took a step back. She didn't like the way he

seemed to only want information about them. "Louse, how much have you told him?"

"Not much," Louse admitted. She rubbed her chin under her shawl. "Just how I see the future and some of my journeys. With each person I talk to, the images are less harsh. Understanding how other cultures comprehend the future really puts things into perspective for me."

"I think we best be going?" Arsenal said. He was holding his yarn again. His eyes glowed slightly brighter as he forced the twine to reveal more of itself than it was prepared for.

"Why the haste?" Michael asked. The eyes that encompassed him began to spin fasted around his torso. "I think there are some things we need to settle."

"Maybe later," Arsenal urged. He grabbed Louse by her arm and motioned for her to follow with wide eyes.

She read the panic in his face and nodded. "It is time then. Goodbye, Michael. It was a joy meeting you. Keep a close eye on that sword of yours."

They started to walk away. Almost home free. Then Michael held up his hand. "Wait."

The Eastreans stopped and exchanged nervous glances.

Michael looked up to the sky and spread his arms as if he was basking in the sun. "But they are so kind. No threat to us... Yes, Lord. I understand, Lord."

He brought his attention back to the Eastreans. His expression was one of pain and confusion. He materialized a sword decorated with gold and silver visages of his home that caught the light like a beacon. "I am sorry but I must follow his will. I advise you bear arms."

Clint Baker

* * * * *

Egypt-Above the Nile

Barrick was at dinner with all of the Egyptian gods aboard the Mandjet. The boat Ra rode across the heavens and hell of his land. He and Barrick called for the summit in hopes to receive aid with the coming threat. He sat next to Ra while Neith sat on his left. The other gods enjoyed the plentiful feast while also murmuring to themselves about the Eastrean and his strange customs.

A grand pool glistened in the sunlight behind them. Blue and white tile created the shapes of flowers around its edge and gods swam freely.

Barrick and Neith flicked berries at each other. They tried to make it into each other's mouths which almost always resulted in being hit in the eye. The giggled with each miss but were persistent in the effort.

Neith caught the last one in her hand. She tossed it into her mouth and motioned at Ra who swished his cup. Barrick nodded in agreement.

"About the extra hands we spoke about before… If you could help us, I would appreciate the effort in any way you can," Barrick said.

"You'll have my aid, friend," Ra said. Jewels of red and blue draped over his shoulders. His white and thinning hair was matted from his sun shaped crown that now rested in front of him. The tan skin on his face wrinkled tightly into an unwavering scrunch. "While most of my pantheon do not wish to admit it, we as gods owe our existence to you. The power that creeps from you is old. With that age comes my respect. Though you look a third of my years."

Ra let out a boisterous laugh then slapped Barrick on the back. He took his gold cup and stood to face his fellow gods. "Let it be known that if Barrick Teal, the Immortal of Reality, calls on you, do as he bids. If not for him, for me and Neith."

Ra, satisfied, sat down to finish his wine. His decree was not met with cheers as he had hoped. Instead, the gods eyed the three at the end of the long table. Behind the crowd, Barrick felt the familiar eyes of Set on him. He was used to the cold glare by now but there was something different in it that he couldn't place.

Barrick was beginning to wonder if he should switch perspectives when Max Sark slammed their tray of meat and fruit next to them.

"You can take your helmet off here, friend," Barrick said. "You're among allies."

Sark scanned the room then shook their head. They signed, "My face is the voices they refuse to see. I do not think they are ready to understand them."

Sark then proceeded to shove the bounty under their helmet. Little bits fell into their lap which worried them none whatsoever.

Barrick turned back to Ra. "Thank you for your support. But I will not ask more than anyone is willing to give."

"They will do as I say," Ra said. "Put your and your wife's worries to rest."

Barrick looked over to his wife. She was tapping her legs and fidgeting with a cup in her lap.

"I'm sorry my love," Barrick said as he took her hand in his. "I was distracted. What is on your mind."

"There's something in the back of my head, Barrick," Neith explained. "Familiar almost. Like we have been here before. *Many* times before."

"We can leave if you like," Barrick offered. "I'm sure Ra will understand."

Neith nodded and Barrick helped her up. He pushed in her chair and took her arm in his.

"We'll be heading home, Ra," he said. "Thank you for everything you have done."

Ra went to object then pointed at Neith, "Will you be okay, Neith? You're looking ill."

Barrick looked back to his wife. It was true. After standing, her face had turned pale and she wobbled on her heals. Barrick took her cup to smell it. He smelled his and Ra's. The molecular structure of the drinks unfolded to him. The faint the traces of…

"Poison," Barrick said. "All of us."

Neith fell to the floor. Only Barrick and Sark rushed to her. Ra stood over them, watching his cohort.

"Who did this then?" Ra yelled. "I burn up toxins in my stomach you idiots. Eastreans digest the molecules and do not feel it's effects."

No one answered. They just stared at him. "Who did this?"

"Hold still, my love," Barrick said while holding her hand. "I'm here. I can save you. I just need to be quick."

Black blood was boring from Neith's mouth, nose, and eyes. She held Barrick's arm as his terrified eyes searched her body. "Take your time, love. I trust you, and will always be with you."

Barrick flicked his eyes, searching for the molecules

that attacked her. With each one, he erased them from existence as if they had never even been created. Simultaneously, he worked on her immune system, building it up so that she could also fight.

Sark backed up Ra. With crossbow drawn, they waved it between gods who only watched.

"Thoth, find Thoth," Ra said. Though no one moved.

From the pool, the surface rippled. Then, without the hint of a warning, the crocodile god, Sobek, lunged from the water, grabbing Barrick and pulling him under.

* * * * *

Greece- Mt. Othrys

The Titans had gathered under the cloudy sky. Their stone thrones were tightly tucked around a long table to match.

Helios, the titan of the sun, looked at the sky. "I don't remember a storm being planned."

Atlas shrugged the comment off. He was the only one to hear. Instead, he stroked his sister's belly. "How much longer do I have to wait for him?"

"Any day now, brother," Calypso said. She smiled and handed Atlas his daughter, also Calypso. "Be patient. As you were with your daughter."

"I was far from patient," Atlas laughed. "In my opinion, Calypso was the most beautiful child to ever be born. Though I may be biased. Have you two settled on a name?"

"Prometheus," Ration said. He smiled with pride. Calypso met his gaze and his smile drifted into a dull grin as he found himself lost in her eyes.

"A strong name!" Atlas roared, breaking their

connection. He took a ham leg from the table and tore a chunk from it. "I will be sure to help him live up to it."

"I appreciate your love," Ration said. He took a sip from his goblet. While he wasn't particularly fond of wine, he drank what was offered. After all, the Eastrean way was to eat and drink what was provided. "I hope you will see him as a brother."

"Silence you two," Cronus boomed. He was at the end of the table. Up until that point he was silent as he watched over his realm. He held his stomach and groaned. "I cannot stand your joviality."

Everyone except Calypso turned to their plates. She nudged her husband who nodded. Ration wasn't scared of Cronus. Compared to him, Cronus was little more than a spoiled king on a mole hill. This did not make him ignorant to the fact that he could hurt those he cared about.

"Cronus," Ration said as he dragged his chair over to him. "A word."

"What is it Eastrean?" Cronus said. He rubbed his belly and winced as he readjusted to face the fire god.

"There's an air of danger," Ration advised. "Louse has told us about various prophecies calling for a great change on the Earth. While we have agreed to not affect the people the gods preside over, we also seek to protect—"

"Get to the point, praiseless," Cronus snapped. He gagged but swallowed what was trying to escape

Ration paid no mind to the insult. Instead, he said, "Can we count on you to fight by our side if the need arises?"

Cronus scratched his beard as he thought on the subject.

Out of the corner of his eye, Ration thought he saw

sparks flicker off a boulder. He started to turn to it when Cronus made his decision.

"We will aid under *my* command," Cronus said. "I can't have a filthy outsider leading ahead of me."

"I can work that," Ration said. He stood to rejoin Calypso. When he sat, Cronus struggled to rise.

"Though I do not care for the fact," Cronus addressed. He burped then gagged. "Ration helped build our kingdom. It is because of this that we will help when called upon. Then consider the Eastreans and Titans even…"

From behind the same boulder, Ration saw a cloak float around to the backside of Cronus' throne. It peaked ever so slightly so that only Ration was able to notice. He was much smaller than the bunch of titans so it was no surprise he wasn't noticed.

"Zeus?" Ration whispered.

"What was that, love?" Calypso asked.

Cronus gagged again as he slammed his hands on the table. Then with one belch, threw up a small woman in a hooded cloak.

Ration focused on Cronus, "I've seen this before. In another life. Pyre is showing it to me."

Then Cronus threw up a man in armor decorated in shells. Then a woman in white robes, then a man in black robes, then finally a woman in grey robes and a wheat crown. All of the youths rose, bewildered by the sudden light.

From around the boulder, Zeus threw aside his robe. His fingers crackled with lighting until a solid bolt emerged. From the peaks, creatures with only one eye tossed weapons to the children that had grown in Cronus' stomach. They eyed them as they filled with the power.

The mountain began to rumbled. From its base, beings with a hundred hands started their climb. They tossed boulders up to prevent anyone from attaching.

Zeus threw a thunder bolt down on his father who shuttered and fell to the ground. Then he saw Ration.

He materialized another bolt and tossed it at Ration. It connected with his chest and though he was able to resist its effects, it arched and connected to Atlas and Calypso behind him.

Ration fell to his knees. He could feel the flames start to consume him but he fought the urge to release back.

"Ration!" Atlas yelled. "Calypso…"

Atlas struggled over to his sister. Ration spun around and took her in his arms. He could hear her heart beat slowing and her breath getting more strained.

"Our son," she said through a cold whisper. "Save our son."

Ration shook his head, then nodded. "I've lived over a trillion lifetimes and I have always loved you in ways that could never fade. Thank you for being the joy I could never replace."

Calypso smiled as she caressed her beloved's face. "I love you too."

Her hand fell with her taking the last look into Ration's eyes.

"Ration, the baby," Atlas said. Tears streamed down his face. He materialized a sword and shield as well as a full set of armor. "I'll make sure you have time."

Ration held Calypso's body tight. A small flame sprouted from his chest and into her stomach. Then she crumbled ashes as a bright light grew then dimmed until all that was left was the baby Prometheus.

It did not cry. Instead, it looked at his father and cooed through golden eyes that grasped for knowledge in the world it was just born into.

Atlas turned to ration to check on him. He saw the flames that began to erupt from Ration's eyes. Realizing what was about to happen, he turned to the titan Iapetus. "Father, take Prometheus and protect him."

The titan ran over to Ration. He took up the baby and reassured Ration by saying, "Like a son if need be."

Iapetus went to fly away but the sea god that was just "born" caught him in a gust of sea water. He went to strike the titan but Ration caught his leg and forced his attention on him.

The sea god had expected the visage of a god but instead was met with a man shaped by flame. The god's shock left just enough of an opening for Iapetus and Prometheus to get away.

Ration slammed the sea god into the ground and threw him from the mountain. Only one thing was on his mind.

Then, in a blast of flames that sent, gods, titans, and monsters flying, Pyre roared, "ZZZEEEEUUUUSSS."

Flood War

Barrick opened his eyes. Water rushed in his ears and nostrils as the crocodile god spun in Ra's pool. With a grip like iron, it took everything Barrick had to break free from the god's attack.

Barrick forced his arm free, then, punched the god under his maw. The force was enough to stun Sobek. He released and started to float away.

Barrick wasn't going to let the god off so easy. He grabbed Sobek by the tail, created platforms under his feet, then lunged out of the water. While in the air, Barrick spun Sobek around and threw him off the boat and back into the Nile. He rolled to the floor next to his friends.

"Neith," Barrick said. He ran over to her and took her hand. "I still have time. I…"

Gods of the Flood

A wave of danger filled him. To the north, he could feel Ration losing control. He had only heard the stories of Pyre but now he could see why Ration stepped out from the fight against War God. "I don't know what to do."

Barrick looked at Neith. The love of his life was depending on him. He looked to where Pyre was growing. Duty was telling him to stop the destruction of another land and its people. His heart pounded. He tried to take the poison out but it was taking too long. He could feel the life draining out of her faster than he could work. He could force it out but there was no telling if she would be able to survive the process.

Then a buzz caught his attention. Several bees flew around his hands and head. They came to a stop and rested on him. Their wings folded so they could dance with comfort on his fingers.

"Trust me," Barrick said.

"Always," Neith managed.

Barrick placed a hand on Neith's head. He pulled the strings that attached her to reality. They glowed as they froze her in the fabric.

"What are you doing?" Ra asked as he deflected a blow from Set. In an upward motion, he caught Set across the chest with his sword. Seeing that he would lose in a prolonged fight, Set jumped from the ship.

Ra reached into his head and ripped out his eye. He threw it at Set as he tried to flee. The eye gained momentum, shifting into a lion headed goddess that slashed at the god across the sky.

Satisfied that the traitorous god couldn't get away, he returned to his friend's side. "Well?"

Clint Baker

"I'm saving her in a backwards kind of way," Barrick said. He pulled at the strings that kept the bees in reality. Then he stitched them together. "She'll transfer the poison over to the bees of the world. I think if I centralize it their stingers then it shouldn't kill them."

"Think?" Ra asked.

"I'm more than positive," Barrick said. "She's frozen in reality right now. It's like she is caught in between existence and impossibility. Neith and bees have always had a connection. This way, I can have her exist in the essence of bees while I go grab Arsenal and back up Ration. The war we have been worried about is here."

Ra shifted his attention to the land of the Titan's. "If Neith trusts you, so do I."

The other gods all fled. Seeing how ferocious Sark fought put a damper on their confidence. They would try again some other day.

Barrick finished his knot. The bees that surrounded him began to glow in a green light. Neith broke apart into trillions of pieces that covered the globe, becoming a part of the insects she held so dear. "She'll be fine for now."

Barrick let out a sigh of relief. "Turn away from me. I need to plane step to Arsenal."

Ra didn't understand it but he did as he was asked. What Ra didn't know was that plane stepping used a person's blind spot to show up behind them. In Barrick's theory, he uses the probability that he is in a position outside of a cognitive plane. While Sark and Ra knew that Barrick was there, they had no way of proving he was until they brought him into their visual plane of reality.

That uncertainty allowed Barrick to switch places with

Carca as she blinked. She had been standing just well enough behind Arsenal that she was outside of both the archangel's field of vision as well as the Baptized, Louse's.

Carca looked around in confusion. The shock of the angel's words still written on her face. "Where... how did I get here."

"Barrick," Sark signed. "The world is falling."

A boom shook the ship. It swayed away from the source yet was able to hold its current path.

From where Ration had made a home, a shadow snaked around the world. Fire emitted from its very essence. Wings and scales engulfed the planet in a red heugh.

Sark fell to the floor. The boards creaked under the weight of his armor. They held their head as the entire world in millions of versions uttered one word over and over. *Dragon*, they said softly. *Dragon*, with more force. *DRAGON,* they screamed into Sark's head.

* * * * *

Barrick ripped Arsenal to the side, he deflected a sword swipe with an Egyptian axe he materialized. It was decorated with bees and symbols Neith and Barrick had created together. In an act that Barrick couldn't explain, it fused to his soul as if it was an extension of his very lifeforce.

"A friend?" Michael asked.

Barrick blinked and sent Louse to Ra the same way he arrived.

Pyre suddenly stretched above them. Michael looked up at the crimson cover. "What is this, Lord?"

Three pillars of light crashed down around them. From

them, stepped three more angels. One ran over to Michael and drew his weapon.

"Gabriel?" Michael asked. "What is the meaning of this?"

"Lucifer," Gabriel said. The same eyes that encircled Michael were around this angel as well. Half were trained on the other angels, the other half on Barrick and Arsenal. "He's leading a war on heaven."

Michael waited for an answer only he could hear. When he had it, he said, "I see. So, it shall be my duty to make sure you are cast out forever."

He leveled his sword at the angel that was beginning to show signs of char around his eyes and horns protruding from his head. "Then forgive me, brother. I must do as I am told."

"This might be our exit," Barrick whispered. He went to plane step to Pyre's head when a blast of light made him and the Immortal of Time dodge out of its redeeming path.

Arsenal's shadow, not getting the clue, took the brunt of the attack. When the light dissipated, it shuttered as it looked for its owner. It drifted over to Arsenal's side on the ground.

"Thanks for having my back," he told it. The shadow paid him no mind.

"I still have my orders with you two," Michael said threw gritted teeth. The overwhelming number of enemies darkened his face.

"Fine then," Barrick said as he rose to his feet. He flipped his axe in his hand then charged with Arsenal close at his heels with a sickle ready in hand. They traded places in their path, then attacked at the same time.

Michael blocked their weapons, then parried to his left.

This made the Immortal's blades slide into each other, creating sparks.

The next thing the angel knew, there were two less enemies to fight. They had disappeared without a trace. The angels all looked at each other in confusion.

The initial shock gone, they charged, bursting into flames and light as their battle took them to heaven.

* * * * *

Sepron opened his eyes from his perch above the world. "That soon…"

The Grave Digger, Etchet, rose from the pig he had been cooking over a fire. Gregorius Mal sniffed the air. His large snout felt a warmth rushing towards them. Then, the neck of Pyre stretched above them.

"HE'S A LOT LARGER THAN I LAST REMEMBER THE STORIES TELLING ME," Etchet said.

"And more powerful," Mal added. He stared at his god in awe.

Warftuff ran out from their pitched tent. "I can't believe it. I can feel the energy. Ration was holding all of this inside him?"

"Forever a growing force," Sepron said. "The wives of Ration and Barrick are dead. I cannot feel their life flowing through them anymore."

"Oh no," Warftuff said. They lowered their head in respect. "Poor Ration. Poor Barrick. I cannot imagine how they are feeling."

"I don't feel Barrick as well," Sepron said. He stood from his rock. "Arsenal is gone too. Curse these lands. Curse this planet and its people and their gods."

"What are you doing?" Mal asked.

Sepron lifted his hand. "Drowning them."

The seas began to rise as if in a cup to Sepron's lips. They spread across the land, slowly eating away at the vast civilizations that grew under the nurturing care of the Eastreans and the other gods.

With each land engulfed, boats, and turtles, and other means of survival braced themselves on the suddenly rising waters.

"Sepron!" the trio behind the god yelled. "Stop!"

"Stop me and I'll drown you too," he snapped. His expression changed to one of regret. As if he had said that phrase thousands of times before. He whispered to a past self, "Or I will drown you too."

The Eastreans froze in their tracks.

"What should we do?" Mal asked.

"THERE," Etchet called. He pointed a hairy finger at a tiny ship that was flying across the skyline. "KATARACT COMES TO US."

The other Eastreans turned to the direction.

"He's coming in rather fast," Warftuff said.

"Too fast," Mal agreed. "Get down!"

Kataract, aboard The Reacher, yanked on the rope that held the sails. He shifted the wind to make the ship grind to a halt above their target.

"Get in!" Kataract yelled. "Blazes if I know what is going on. We'll soon to find out together."

The bulls, Baller and Baller, peaked over the edge of the ship. They were swishing their tails as if this was the best fun they had in years.

Gods of the Flood

They mooed at the Eastreans as if to say, "Heeeellllloooo, miiighty fine day we're having, iiiisn't it."

The rest of the Baptized in Fire and Grave Diggers helped their comrades onto the deck. Kataract had picked up a few other creatures in his travels since the last they saw the ship. They manned a few of the sails and sat with weapons ready.

Tristan sat at a tiny forge making arrows for the crew's bows. He muttered, "Not again, we can't go through this again." Over and over as he made sure they had plenty on hand.

"Sepron," Kataract yelled over the railing. "Are you coming."

Sepron flipped his hand. A gust of wind sent the ship flying across the sky. Everyone held on screaming. The exceptions were Baller and Baller who mooed in delight.

Asha rushed over to a sail and tied it down to a rail on the port side. This gave Kataract enough room to pull the right rope and balance the ship.

"We need Barrick and Arsenal," Kataract said. "We need to stop our gods."

"Sepron said they were gone," Mal informed. "But he said it like they had just disappeared and weren't dead. I know Barrick was with the Egyptians. Start there."

"Right," Kataract said. He turned the ship around. He peered over the rigging where he noticed the night moon crossing the sky. "He's going to be busy. I'm sorry I can't help more, old friend."

Kataract caught the right current and sent them hurdling across to a situation unknown.

Clint Baker

* * * * *

Contrary to the current belief, Barrick and Arsenal were not dead. As it turned out, when they combined their efforts, they could cross time and space together to alternate realities. A secret they would have to discover together.

About an hour after they disappeared in front of the angels, they popped back into existence.

"Where was that place?" Arsenal asked.

"Earth to be sure," Barrick said.

"I understand that but there…"

"Were no gods on it," Barrick confirmed. He snapped his fingers and an apple formed in it. "I feel stronger knowing that. Like I need to protect what we know."

Arsenal remembered a conversation he had with Gender God once. *It is a shame you two aren't considered gods. By Eastrean standards you are as close to gods they come. You out shine any god here on Earth by eons.*

"We need to get back," Arsenal said. Water was beginning to seep from the sands. It swirled around their ankles in a cascade of forewarning.

"And fast," Barrick said. He searched the horizon for the other Eastreans. All of which were aboard Kataract's ship.

He grabbed Arsenal by the wrist, twisted him out of eyeshot and plane stepped on board The Reacher.

"Barrick, Arsenal," Warftuff gasped. They hugged the immortals with a force of worry. "Sepron said you two were gone. I knew that couldn't be right. Where did you go?"

The duo exchanged glances that told the each other the same thing, don't give too much.

"We don't know," Barrick lied. "We blinked out of

existence for a while. I'm happy you all are safe. What's the situation?"

"We've been fighting gods all day," Kataract said. "They blame us for the world flooding. Which is true."

Barrick twisted his head in confusion.

"Sepron," Carca said. She was rubbing her arms and looking at the forming clouds. "He's upset with how this world has turned out."

"He's wiping it clean?" Arsenal said with shock. "Where is Trilo?"

"Below deck," Tristan said. "He's far too weak to do anything."

"And Pyre took over Ration," Barrick noted. "We need a plan."

The Eastreans looked for answers from Arsenal and Barrick. They realized that the time had come for them to lead again.

"Right," Arsenal said. "I forgot."

"Sark. Carca," Barrick commanded. "Can you two bring Ration back?"

"I suppose I can make something to put Pyre to sleep," Carca said. "It'll take most of my Eastrean plants but I'll start working on it now."

She ran below deck to start the project.

"I've heard some lullabies on the winds," Sark signed. They had meant a word between air and rumor but didn't have the sign for it. "Perhaps that could be of some help."

"That was what I was hoping, thank you friend." Barrick turned to the remaining Eastreans. "It'll be our job to back them up. The world is angry and there is no telling what challenges we are going to face."

"We're behind you," Kataract said. "Lead us true."
"Kataract," Arsenal said. "Take us to Pyre's head."

* * * * *

Sark and Carca rolled onto Pyre's nose. They slid against his scales until their boots a confident grip. Carca made sure her tucked wings so the raging winds didn't throw her from the surface. They waved to The Reacher to signal that they were fine. It caught the appropriate winds and was off.

"Let's get to the end," Sark signed. "From there I should be able to be close enough to you to help if needed. Then I'll tap into Pyre's thoughts to perform the lullaby."

"Sounds good," Carca said.

They planted their feet and traversed the scales. The heat that emitted from the creation god would have made any mortal burn. Thanks to Ration's protection, however, this wouldn't be the case for the Immortals of Language and Medicines.

At the tip of the nose, Carca planted a spike and rope. This gave no sensation to the god. They couldn't even tell if the god noticed them. Carca tried not to think about that fact as she descended.

According to Ration, Pyre once spanned half the entirety of the universe. It was only by chance that he struck the spark of life.

"Not even half his size," Carca said to herself.

Sark placed their hands on Pyre and closed their eyes. They could feel the hum of existence rushing through the god.

Sark thought of Ra. They hoped the sun god was okay.

Gods of the Flood

The last thing the Immortal of Languages heard from him, he was fighting to regain control of his pantheon. They couldn't imagine what the lands were going through. First, they were scorched by the eye of Ra and then flooded.

Sark put their worries aside. *Focus.*

They looked into Pyre's mind. It was nearly impossible to navigate. His mind was more so a force than a language but still had formation.

Not words, feelings, Sark noticed. They changed the songs. Instead, they thought, *Comfort. Warmth, not burning, warmth. Security, love...*

At love, Pyre shook. Sark saw the images of pain and heartbreak. The image of Calypso flashed in their mind. They saw the life her and Ration had tried to build. The future robbed from them. Her in his arms as she faded away to give life to their son.

Sark's eyes started to tear and drip from their helmet. *Security, safety, friendship.*

Ration fought back before easing. Sark saw all the pain Ration had been carrying. The guilt of a fallen world. The weight of nations perishing under his watch. With each bad thought, Sark reassured the god until his mind was calm enough to give Carca her shot.

Carca slid down her rope using a pulley system Tristan made her. She used her wings to guide the winds around her so that they didn't make the drop too difficult.

She stopped in the center of Pyre's left nostril. She tied herself around the waist to free both of her hands. She then took out a vial and wiped a green substance on several crossbow bolts.

The substance was made out of all Eastrean

ingredients: Sea stone for muscle tension, black canter flowers for drowsiness, drope (a lizard that once roamed Eastrea), bone marrow for peaceful sleep, and various other plants that were known to cause almost immediate sleep.

She loaded the bolts into her crossbow, took aim, then fired the entire cylinder into the depths. Satisfied that all had found a mark inside the giant god, she pulled herself up to sounder footing.

At Sark's side, she offered words of encouragement. "That is all we can do. Keep it up."

Sark didn't acknowledge her. They wanted to sign an insult about *what do you think I'm trying to do,* but didn't have the available hands to do so.

Pyre began to rumble. His eyes blinked slower and slower until they could no longer open. Then, as suddenly as he formed, Pyre disappeared, sending the Immortals into a dead fall.

Carca spun her wings around so that she was facing the ground. Sark was falling at a greater rate than she was so she ducked into a dive.

She reached out her hand and grabbed Sark by the back of the neck. She tucked them under her belt and told them, "Hold on to my hip, help me find Ration."

The rising ocean was in bound as they plummeted. It wasn't until they breached the clouds that Sark saw Ration fully unconscious falling beside them.

They tapped Carca then pointed at their god. Carca leveled her wings to match Ration's speed. She reached her arms out and scooped him from the sky.

The weight of her friends was starting to wear on her, but Carca slowed their fall as much as she could. Her wings were not built for flying but for gliding and the extra effort proved it.

"Kataract!" she yelled. She closed her eyes against the weight. "We're here!"

From the clouds peaked The Reacher. It turned on its bow and dove for the three falling voyagers. When it was under them at a comfortable distance, it turned up, landing them on its deck.

"You did it," Arsenal said. He ran and scooped up his friend. "We were lucky this time."

"Lucky?" Trilo said. He emerged from below deck. "Look at the world. Look at Ration. How is this lucky?"

"We're alive," Barrick said. "We're handling every situation one at a time. Now we just need to get Sepron to stop and—"

"And then what?" Trilo yelled. "He caused all of this. He put his trust in foreign gods. Gods *you* created, Barrick. I should destroy you and Reality's Bend. An Immortal should not have the power you two do. You shouldn't be as powerful as me."

Barrick tried to read the faces on The Reacher but none gave help. "Trilo, we hear your concerns. We can address them later. We have more pressing matters to attend to. Sepron—"

"Is right," Trilo interrupted. He propped himself up against the front mast. "This world has run amuck. Eastrea never had these many problems."

"Eastrea never had this many types of people," Tristan said. He was tending to Ration up until this point. "I trust Ration and his wisdom. The actions of other gods shouldn't be his weight."

"They respond to him," Trilo said. "To his actions. To his presence. He's asleep now and I say now is the time to bring mercy on the world."

The Eastreans all stepped in between Trilo and Ration.

"Trilo, please," Arsenal urged. "Let's put this aside for now. We can make better plans and rules later. For now, we have to fix—"

Trilo charged Arsenal. He tackled the Immortal of Time under the belt and lifted him up, then over the side of the ship.

"Arsenal!" Barrick yelled. He ran over to the edge to see where they were falling. He turned to the Eastreans who waited for his command. "Get to Sepron. Convince him to stop the flood. I'll get them and rejoin you."

Specks behind them caught Barrick's eye. Gods by the thousands were descending upon them.

"They're coming for us," Barrick said as he pointed. "Get Ration below deck and protect him at all costs."

"Right," the Eastreans all said.

Barrick went to jump when Kataract caught him by the shoulder. "He made a promise to me once that he couldn't keep. Promise me that you will get them back."

"That's what I do," Barrick said. "Protect them."

Kataract saluted Barrick, then took the helm.

Barrick took another look at Arsenal and Trilo falling. He threw himself over, blinked, then forced a plane step just behind them.

They slammed into him, sending everyone spiraling. Trilo summoned his hammer. He tried to swing it at Barrick but did little more than tap him. Barrick wedged himself between the two, then pushed.

Trilo separated, only then realizing where he was. He pointed at the ground and pulled upward, making a mountain stretch up and catch him in the earth. It crumbled away, leaving a small island for the god to stand on.

Barrick grabbed ahold of Arsenal under his arm. He waved his hand in a circle. The water parted, then formed the glowing green strings of reality. He rewrote the particles that made it up so that they acted more like a soft rubber net. They hit the surface with little impact, broking into the vastness that was the oceans.

They continued to sink. Barrick held his breath as he searched for Trilo. Instead, he was met with a creature beyond his understanding. Its giant humanoid body stared at them through the eyes of something that resembled an octopus. Its slimy skin sent shivers down Barrick's spine.

It tried to reach out to the Immortals but Barrick shook his head. He could hear its intent for them. To take them and make them one of its own.

It tried to invade The Immortals mind but Barrick stitched a rule into its reality. *No corrupting beings of influence.*

Realizing it was outmatched, the creature swam away with its webbed hands and toes creating new currents around it.

Barrick and Arsenal fell to the ocean floor. Fish flopped as they struggled to breath in their new environment.

Barrick looked up. "Sepron is lifting the oceans. I would never have imagined."

Arsenal spit up water. "I could. I saw it. I didn't believe it then but I saw it in our history and now I *have* to believe it."

"He's not going to come with us," Barrick realized.
"Not easily anyway," Arsenal added.
"One more fight," Barrick sighed.
"Let's get it over with," Arsenal said. He stretched his shoulders, legs, and arms. He then summoned his sickles.

Barrick summoned his axe. He rubbed the symbol for Neith and prayed that he was right. He spun back-to-back with Arsenal and plane stepped them to the top of the new ocean. They hovered over the waves just enough for Barrick to flatten the water's surface. They landed without a problem.

The ocean crashed against the perfect rectangle oceanwater slab frozen in time. They looked around for Trilo with weapons at the ready.

The ocean split, pushing the Immortals back. Out formed a small island with Trilo at its peak. He stumbled as it settled. With a great heave he stood up straight, let his hammer slide down his hand, then threw it over his shoulder.

"I might not have much energy," he said. "But I have enough to deal with you two."

Trilo lunged himself forward. An effort he wasn't aware would weigh on him. He tried to slam into Arsenal, but Barrick slammed him first.

Trilo used the land he brought from the ocean to drift in a wide circle, then propelled himself back to the Immortals. Barrick being the target this time.

Barrick ducked under a hammer swing. He flung his axe behind him. It bounced off the hammer's head and went flying into the ocean.

Barrick pulled the strings of reality to spell out "back". The axe spun out of the water, narrowly missing Trilo's nose and landed back into Barrick's hand.

Gods of the Flood

Trilo stumbled onto some stones. He tried to summon more land but found that only a few boulders would surround him. This gave Barrick just enough room to summon a full platform of stationary under his feet. It flattened a hundred-foot wave that pushed him up to its peak, then dropped him onto the stone god.

Trilo went to block with the hilt of his hammer as Barrick brought down his axe, embedding itself deep into the ancient wood. Under the pressure of the two forces, the axe carried all the way through the hilt, embedding into Trilo's third eye.

Trilo gripped the eye and yelled in pain. The blood that ran from his fingers dripped into the ocean, making it muddy and thick. He looked at his hammer head, now just barely long enough to hold with one hand. He then threw the hilt at Barrick who caught it in his other hand.

It radiated with power. He could feel the splinters in the wood calling to him to claim them. "Just come back, Trilo. Carca can heal you on The Reacher... then all will be forgiven. We are all a little panicked. I'm sure everyone will understand."

"I don't want to go back to a group that feels obligated to follow me," Trilo yelled. "And I don't want them to. Especially you and the Immortal that can't even keep track of his own shadow."

Arsenal looked under his feet where his shadow was indeed late yet again. "He moves in a constant state of confusion in the right direction. That is just a small quirk of our existence. All of us have one. Come back so that we may celebrate our differences and be stronger."

"I'd rather see you two crushed." Trilo snapped his

fingers. One of the boulders that surrounded him fell into the depths of the churning currents. "Consider this my resignation from the Eastreans."

From the depths, rose a shadow. It separated the ocean between the Immortals and the god as it sat up waist deep. The colossal looked at the three miles below it, then stood.

It spoke in a language the Immortals couldn't make out. They assumed it was asking for orders. With each word, stone and dust fell from its lips.

"Defend me!" Trilo yelled to it.

The colossal stood from the ocean, shifting the currents around it as it did so.

"Barrick?" Arsenal said, trying his hardest to keep his feet planted. The worry in his eyes told volumes to the Immortal of Reality.

Barrick tried to force their platform around the colossal but it slammed its hand down and pushed the two back, sending them several miles from their target.

Barrick forced his platform closer, this time avoiding the hands and heading straight under his feet. The colossal shifted its legs and a mountain of waves pushed Barrick back.

Barrick forced the platform around to Arsenal and joined them together. He turned to his friend. "We'll need to beat the giant first. Unless you have any ideas?"

"None," Arsenal admitted. "How do we kill it?"

Barrick stared at the colossal's head. It was arched down at them at just the right angle so that the sun's brightness blinded them.

"I can perform a perception clap," Barrick suggested.

"A what?" Arsenal asked. He shifted as he tried to look through the colossal.

Barrick closed one eye and expanded his index finger and his thumb. He opened and closed them around the giant. "I'd have to be high up for that."

He stared at the sun through his finger tips, "Really high up."

Arsenal shifted nervously at the Immortal of Reality, "Barrick? What are—"

"I'm going to throw you," Barrick said with a nod.

"You're going to what?" Arsenal exclaimed.

Barrick grabbed Arsenal under the armpits, "Just trust me. Keep your eyes closed and when you feel a push, you're on your own for a moment."

"Barrick, no. Barrick!" Arsenal argued just before being throw straight up. He soared through the air until he was at the giant's belt.

"Not high enough," Barrick said. When e plane stepped behind Arsenal, he grabbed him by the hand, spun them both, then threw the Immortal even higher.

This time, it was perfect. Arsenal was now just above the colossal who reached out for Arsenal. Barrick plane stepped again, this time, so high that the colossal was barely the size of an ant in perspective.

Barrick closed his left eye. He then kicked his left foot into view of his right eye and over Arsenal. The Immortal of Reality then used the gap between them to snag Arsenal with the strings of reality and drug him across the sky and out of the way.

To Arsenal, there was a sudden tug that sent him miles from Trilo and his monster. He skipped across the water, struggling to find a way to make himself stop.

Barrick thrust out his hands to initiate the perception

clap. He took his left hand so that it looked like the colossal was on his palm. He held his right hand high above it. Keeping his left eye closed, Barrick clapped his hands together.

To Barrick, little more than the sound of a clap and a light crunch was all that he could perceive. This could not be said for Trilo.

On his last boulder, Trilo saw the Immortals fly through the air and in between the waves disappear. Once Barrick reached his peak, the god's beloved colossal exploded into a second flood of blood. Defenseless, he was caught up in it.

The waves pushed him down as the crimson fused together with the salt water. The currents drug the god away screaming for air and land that refused to come to him.

As Barrick fell, he searched for Arsenal. The Immortal of Time froze himself in the moments before he descended far the water. Using the moment, Barrick plane stepped behind him, then grounded his friend so that he may return.

Arsenal snapped out of the state, shaking. "Never, do that again."

"If I can help it." Barrick sighed. "Are you okay?"

"Besides being thrown across the planet?" Arsenal stammered, I'm fine. Where's Trilo?"

"Gone," Barrick said. "The colossal's blood drowned him."

Barrick reached out for Reality's Bend which he had left in Egypt. He grabbed the strings that held it in place and pulled it toward them.

The two collapsed onto the new platform Barrick created. They used the moment to catch their breath as the currents pushed them to worlds beyond what they knew.

* * * * *

Kataract let the sails drop The Reacher into a nose dive. While Baller and Baller slid across the deck on their rear ends, mooing with glee, the other Eastreans braced themselves against the onslaught of gods.

They rode on chariots, mounts, and the winds as they released volleys of various weapons and power. Tristan stayed hard at work creating arrows and weapons for those of the crew that could not handle the Eastrean's encumbering weapons. With each batch, he would yell out the names of Kataract's crew who would abandon their post for just enough of an edge to keep them in the fight.

Carca and Sark were back-to-back. Every time a god would land on the deck, they would quickly dispatch with a sword swing, crossbow bolt, or simple hand to hand. When each god fell, they released a gust of essence from their domains.

The Baptized in fire had formed a shield wall on the port side. Every time a god would show itself, they would release a volley of bolts that would send it falling into the ocean.

"We need to get to Sepron," Warftuff yelled to Kataract.

"I'm trying," he gasped. He twisted a rope around his left arm and yanked. The ship lurched to the right, narrowly avoiding a god with eight arms.

Asha was at the helm. With each movement of the sails, she would spin the wheel in the appropriate direction to help guide them through the air. She couldn't help but notice the muscles and bones in Kataract's arms and shoulders creaking with each change of the sails.

She had known he was big but didn't realize until she had seen the other Eastreans fighting around them just how dense of a man Kataract was. Even Lanta, the smallest of the Eastreans, matched Asha in height. Looking back at the Immortal of Currents now, she saw that he towered at least an extra foot above them all.

A wind god materialized behind them. Kataract made the motion to make The Reacher fall into a nose dive again. He stopped himself when he realized who it was.

"Vayu?" Asha stumbled over the wheel but quickly regained her composure.

The wind god landed next to Kataract and patted him on the shoulder. "The world has fallen into chaos. They say you all are to blame?"

"We don't know the full details yet but at least the flood is our fault," Kataract admitted.

Another god with wings and a bow and quiver landed next to them.

"Passion god too?" Kataract said. "I wish we weren't so popular.

"They call me Eros now," the god said. "At least this part of me?"

"Noted," Kataract said as he strained to avoid a golden chariot.

The gods exchanged looks as they sized each other up.

"We'll watch your back," Eros decided.

"Though it looks like you might not need the support," Vayu added. He motioned at Sark who shot bolts into a fire god's knees, then leaped over him while the Immortal of Languages tore his head off in one fluid motion.

"Who trained you Eastreans?" Vayu asked.

"Life," Eros said as he launched an arrow into a forest god. "They created everything. All of this. You don't live that long unless you have the experience to keep you alive."

Vayu lowered his eyes. He realized that his suspicions were correct. These Eastreans could end the world on a whim if they had decided to. He didn't get the impression that they would, however. He read survival and desperation on their faces. A deep desire to exist alongside everyone.

The wind god knew this was a foolish dream for them to have. It wasn't in human nature. There was a reason all of the gods present didn't get along. Why they were fighting now. He himself had just left the battle from his own continent where hurricanes and tornadoes fought against them. If even his own gods couldn't see eye-to-eye, how could the Eastreans expect others accept them?

"Carca," Kataract yelled. He let the ropes slip to allow the winds to catch the sails enough to lift the ship up. "Is there any way to wake Ration? We'll need him if there's any way to stop Sepron."

She looked over to Sark who shrugged. "We can try."

"Try it quick then," Kataract struggled. He threw the ropes in his right hand over to his left. The ship shifted as he did so but maintained its stability. Several gods landed behind him, forcing Kataract, Vayu, and Eros to fight them off.

Carca turned on her heals, grabbed Sark who swung their sword wildly, and dragged them below deck where Ration slept.

To make up for the lack of Immortal help, the Baptized

formed into smaller groups while maintaining smaller shield domes. Lanta, Wallace, and Warftuff formed one group. Bullio, Louse, and Mal another. Alex and Flass together on the last. They circled around each other, letting out volleys of bolts that left little room for a direct attack.

A wind god slammed into the side of The Reacher, sending the Baptized scattering like marbles across the deck. They struggled to regain their footing as he yanked the ship back and forth.

Warftuff hit the railing then flipped over the side. Wallace grabbed ahold of their hand and started to pull them back on board.

An ice god flew under them, then blew chilled air on them. Warftuff wiggled and kicked as they tried to fight the breeze but was encased in a block of ice before they had a chance to respond.

With the sudden biting frost, Wallace was forced to let go. He swung his other hand down to try to catch his friend but was just out of reach.

Ida Lanta leaped over him and caught the ice, giving Wallace just enough space to catch her leg. He looked up and saw three gods racing towards him.

"Kataract," he yelled. The Immortal had found himself in an eight vs three fight and wouldn't be able to help.

"Alex." All of the Baptized were in their own fights.

"Anyone?" No one was around that could help.

Wallace could feel Ida starting to slip. He braced his stomach so that he could use both hands.

"Let me go," Ida Lanta said. "I can glide us down. Everyone needs you."

"I need you too," Wallace begged.

"I can fly and ice floats. Let go, Nathanial!" Lanta kicked his hands with enough force to allow her thin leg to break free. "I'll find you. I promise."

She fell no less than thirty feet before the wind god that had hit the ship blasted her with a current. Ida was forced to let go of Warftuff but was sure to keep her eye on them.

The god scooped her up but was unable to hold on to her. Lanta maneuvered her way to the gods back and snapped his neck. The god then exploded into a hundred winds that caught the flaps of her skin and pushed her upward.

As she floated, she scanned the sky for Warftuff. The former general had fallen faster than she thought and had just crashed into the giant ocean. They submerged momentarily then broke the surface.

She sighed with relief. At least that way they could get back to them. She started to glide back to The Reacher when another god plucked her out of the sky.

Wallace watched helplessly as she fought and killed the many gods that were stupid enough to think that she was an easy target.

"You better find me," Wallace finally said. He turned back to the rest of the Eastreans. They were winning, there was no doubt in his mind about that. He slapped the horns on his head and charged.

* * * * *

It was Carca who was able to awaken Ration. He rubbed his eyes where the last flickers of Pyre's fire extinguished. Instead, there was a darkness in his face. It was like his life had been taken from him. He had a far off look in his eyes as if he was lost in a moment that just would not allow him to leave. A monster of another kind

Carca hugged Ration though he did not hug her back. The usual warmth she had felt the last time she embraced him was gone. Now it almost hurt her to as all kindness had drained from him.

"We need your help," Sark signed. They explained what was going on in the world and what Sepron and Pyre had done. "He's the only one who will listen to you."

"I'm sure you can solve it on your own," Ration said. He stretched out onto his hammock. He went to close his eyes when Carca grabbed him.

"We tried! I'm sorry about Calypso but we *need* you. Barrick and Arsenal are fighting Trilo and don't forget that Barrick lost his wife too. None of us are strong enough to fight Sepron and he doesn't respect any of us enough to stop. You can mourn when the day is over, Ration. For now, be the man I know you are and bring us all together again."

Ration sighed. He opened a portal to Sepron and the three stepped inside.

Sepron was up to his knees in water. Etchet had disappeared to be with the other Gravediggers.

"Sepron," Ration said. "That's enough."

"Look at what they've done," Sepron said. "Do they not deserve it."

"The world?" Ration asked. "No. We created this world whether we like it or not so that is enough. I will not tolerate the destruction of another world."

"We'll still live," Sepron said.

Ration grabbed Sepron by the shoulder. He put his index and middle fingers onto the water god's head. The god dropped his arms. His eyes flickered as Ration rewrote the god's personality. He replaced hatred and anger with love and compassion.

The water around their legs began to recede and swirled back to the original height.

Carca and Sark looked at each other. Had he always been able to do that?

He turned back to them. "There. I fixed it."

Ration closed his eyes and forced his thoughts into the minds of all deities including the Eastreans. "Attention all gods. Cease our fights and find me. It has become clear that we are in need of some rules if we are to continue moving forward. I will make my presence known to all of you. Find me."

Gods around the world froze. In the wars that shook the world, they all felt a sense of fear wash over them as they realized how little control they had over the world. This god controlled it all and they knew that it would be by his word that he allowed them to exist. They laid down their arms and vanished to collect their thoughts amongst themselves.

He brought his attention to the Immortals. "I'll protect you but we'll have to make some sacrifices to resolve the damage we've done. Then I'll need some time to think."

They saluted their god. Unsure about how they felt about him now, all they could do was wait.

* * * * *

Trilo heard the call but ignored the order. He was too weak to return to face the fire god. He pulled himself up. Mud and blood splattered his armor and skin so that he was little more than a lost soul. He unbuckled his armor that disappeared into the ether of the world. He would never realize the armor had a new owner in Graphite who had secured the Icarian forces in a tomb of stone just before the floods hit.

Trilo rubbed his third eye that was melded into his forehead. It would never open again. He analyzed his war hammer and its short hilt. "Just you and me."

Ida Lanta saw him first. She glided herself down next to her god and helped him up. She was covered in the multicolored blood of gods from all the cultures that had attacked her.

"Trilo," She gasped. "I'm so happy I found you. We were worried we would never get you back. Let's head to Kataract. He can take us to—"

Trilo stopped her rambling short by clutching her throat. He squeezed tighter as she struggled to get away. "Let me make this clear to you and all others of this world. I will *never* be an Eastrean again. I renounce my name and all titles I once had. I am now... Odin... and I will raise my own pantheon to challenge yours."

Ida punched the god as he squeezed even tighter than before. Her body snapped free of life as the god crunched her neck and threw her to the side.

He took in a deep breath, then let it out. He let his hammer guide him.

* * * * *

1 week later

It was Wallace and Mal who found Ida Lanta. Her body was sunken in the mud so that her lifeless eyes stared up at them.

Wallace wept as he lifted her up and out. He scrubbed the mud out of her hair as the tears fell onto her skin. Her neck was bruised from where she was killed.

Mal sniffed the air and the ground to find the god that killed her's trail.

"That can't be right," Mal whispered to himself. He sniffed her and the ground again. While there were several hundred gods on her scent, only one had been in the area. Trilo.

Han Bullio joined them. "We need to get to the summit."

Mal ran over to him and asked the Baptized to check the area again. He did and confirmed that the one had at least been with Ida when she died was in fact Trilo. They told Wallace their findings.

"Arsenal and Barrick failed," he said. He handed Ida to Gregorius Mal as if he was handing him thin glass. "Get her back. I'll handle him."

"Wallace, just come back with us," Mal pleaded.

"Wallace is right," Bullio said. "I'll join you."

"You don't have—"

"I want to," Bullio interrupted. "You lost your closest friend and I lost an ally. Let us finish what others couldn't. Go, Mal. We'll catch up."

Mal looked at his friends. Their eyes were sunken and weary from the previous day's fight. They hadn't slept since Ration called for the summit. "I am not the strongest. Or the most important of the Baptized… If you two don't come back it would leave a hole in us that could never be filled. Be careful."

Wallace lowered his head. Tears were still streaming down his face at the thought of losing another friend after the eons they had spent together.

He put his helmet on to hide his bloodshot eyes from the others. He saluted Mal with nothing but pride. "We will be back."

Bullio laughed then saluted. His trunk lifted to the sky and he let out his best elephant bugle. "I'll bring him home, Mal. No need to worry."

Mal lowered his eyes. He turned from them so that they wouldn't see his worry. "I love you all, you know. Not in a romantic way of course. In the way that I worry and care for your happiness. I hope that revenge sets your minds at ease. If it is Trilo, just come home."

He trotted away with Ida Lanta in his arms. His heart ached more with every step he took away from Wallace and Bullio.

They turned to Trilo's trail. They stretched and eyed the horizon with determination. In the way only those who have survived together can understand, they marched to settle what tore away at their souls.

* * * * *

Barrick ran into Reality's Bend with Arsenal close on his heels. The Floods had subsided but Barrick's urgency baffled the Immortal of Time.

"We won, Barrick," Arsenal urged. "We don't need to rush. Let's just head to Ration and see what he has to say."

"First thing's first," Barrick said. He slammed open the final door in the corridor to rolling hills littered with flowers.

Gods of the Flood

A town had started to develop. There were no inhabitants though it seemed like it was move in ready.

"You've been busy," Arsenal noted.

"Neith and I have been building a sort of haven," Barrick explained. "People have been writing and we thought that some of their stories would end up here. That's why we built them a home. The bees are our hobby."

Arsenal hadn't noticed them until mentioned. Thousands of bees started to swarm around their legs as they danced from flower to flower. They had an unnatural attraction to Barrick as he walked with ease among them. Arsenal wasn't so lucky. He strained to avoid accidently stepping on one.

Barrick made his way into the center of a valley that rested between the largest hill and one that overlooked the town of Reality's Bend. He raised his hand up and crooked his fingers. The bees left their busy lives to come to him. They created a tornado of buzzes that shook the fields as it grew.

One landed on Arsenal, then another and another. He lifted up his arms to take a closer look. He realized that they weren't the same species. Some were smaller with greyer tones while others were large and fat with yellow and black stripes. Every combination of color and design was here only leaving room for Arsenal to watch in awe.

"Barrick, what are you doing?" he called.

"Neith was poisoned right before Ration changed," Barrick explained. "I put her essence in all of the bees of the world and made sure the poison was divided up evenly among them in their stingers."

"Oh…" Arsenal said. He took a step back. The swarm had grown into an incomprehensible number.

They started to glow with the green light of reality as

Barrick grabbed on to their strings. He made the same stitch he did before, then pulled.

The bees all shook and fell before resuming their pattern around the Immortal of Reality. He tilted his head and made the stitch again, this time sending a thread through to unravel it. With this pull the bees fell again and swarmed again.

He tried every way possible. He could see the threads that lead to Neith but they had become intertwined so tightly with the bees of the world that she was part of their reality. To take her away would be like taking away all protection and necessity they held.

Barrick dropped to the grass. The bees flew around him then dispersed on the breeze that blew through the hills. He sat while staring at the vast echoes only his eyes could see.

Arsenal ran up to him. "Barrick! What happened?"

Barrick turned his head to his friend. Tears streamed his face and his lip quivered as he tried his hardest not to break down. The tears blinded him as he tried to explain. "I can't... I can't bring her back... It's permanent. I can hear her people telling her stories but she isn't with them. She isn't with me. She isn't with me..."

Arsenal embraced Barrick. He hugged the Immortal of Reality into his chest while holding the back of his head. "It's okay, Barrick. Break down. Let it out. Don't hold it. I had no idea you were bearing so much weight today. You were so strong and I had no idea just how strong. Let me help bear the weight for a while."

Barrick did just that. He wept into his friend, clutching at his only source of reality. That this was his truth now. The wails shook the halls of Reality's Bend. Had he not been inside, the entire world would hear his cries for forgiveness.

* * * * *

Ration built himself a throne of magma and brimstone. Its smoke rose to the sky as a beacon for all seeking him out. His left leg was propped on the arm rest and the same sided arm rested on his knee cap.

Baller and Baller rested on either side. Their snores rumbled the throne as they dreamed of the past day's events.

Gods from every region of the world littered the small valley. Most of the Eastreans sat at a long stone table that accommodated all of them. Ration looked down at them.

"Where's Barrick?" he asked Arsenal.

"He'll be along shortly," Arsenal informed. "He has been composing himself after the fight. It was short but hard on him."

"I see. And Trilo?" Ration asked with the raise of the eyebrow. "How did you two deal with him?"

Arsenal scanned for helpful faces where he found only battle hardened and tired stares. "We couldn't bring him back. He's resigned his position as one of our gods. He might have drowned though we can't tell for sure."

Ration's eyes somehow saddened even further. He looked at Alex, Flass and Louse. "I'm only seeing you three. Where are Warftuff, Lanta, Mal, Wallace, and Bullio?"

The Baptized exchanged glances as they silently argued on who should answer. It was Flass who spoke up. "We don't know. Mal and Wallace were tracking down Lanta. Then Bullio had a bad feeling and decided to track them down. Warftuff is lost and we were going to put efforts into finding them after the meeting."

Ration scratched the stubble that formed on his face. He searched his thoughts and memories. "Leave Warftuff be. I'll find them. Even if it's in another life."

"Why have you called us here?" Zeus boomed as he approached the Eastreans. "We were winning!"

The Eastreans all drew their arms and surrounded their gods.

Sparkes ignited behind Zeus's cold and malice filled smile. "Did I strike a nerve?"

"You killed my wife!" Ration snapped. "It is only by my control, patience, and forgiving nature that you still draw breath."

Zeus took a step back. "Y—you forgive me? What kind of all-powerful god forgives so easily."

"One who knows what vengeful actions create for the world," Graphite said. He erupted from the ground with the bear-like Icarian he saved with Ration and Trilo and a wolf like Icarian at his back. Seeing the second, Flass, Alex, and Louse all murmured to each other. They had the feeling that they knew him from some distant place. "I stand with the Eastreans on this matter. I have the feeling they're more concerned with the world than they are with the actions of gods who didn't know any better."

"I knew exactly what I was doing," Zeus huffed.

"Yet you don't know the restraint shown to you," Graphite urged. "Ration has the power to break apart this world in a single swing. Do you really thing yourself so strong that you could do any harm to him? Me perhaps but him?"

Zeus shot Ration a glance. If this is how the god's enemies revered him, how far would his allies go? "I have your son. What was his name again? Prometheus?"

Flames began to erupt from Ration's eyes before subsiding again. "It is unwise to threaten me. You kill my son, I will do more than kill you Zeus. Remember that I have the capability to make sure you never even existed. I trust you will take good care of him while I right some of my wrongs here. I cannot forget that you did a service to the world by taking care of Cronos. You might have beaten him with ease, do not take me for the rat he is. Bears do not care for the vermin that inhabit their cave."

"We were here first," Zeus said.

This sent an uproar among the gods of the world. They all bore arms as they argued about who were the ones to create Earth, the cosmos, and the universe.

"Silence!" Eros said. "I am a primordial force and I have seen wars between gods far older than any of you. The Eastreans predate even that. It is to my understanding that the Immortal, Barrick Teal, is the reason we all can exist as we do."

"I saw the one you are speaking of fight," a god with a red painted face said. "He altered reality on his whim. In ways none of us can and have the capability to. He is far more powerful any of us can manage."

"If we are to continue as we do," the archangel Michael said. "There should be some equalizers. I represent my god in this matter. Even he, who is in all and is all would be powerless against them. Should such power exist on our world? How many gods fell to you Eastreans and how many of your own rank?"

The Eastreans counted among themselves. They totaled over three-hundred gods between them. They then admitted that only Warftuff was known to be unaccounted for. The hills fell silent at the realization.

"It is because of our power that I called for this meeting," Ration said. "I call that all supernatural forces should not affect the world or the areas outside of their respective regions. The souls of the innocent are the cost of war amongst us."

"They are there to serve us," a god with a lion head said.

"You all exist because of humanity," Arsenal said. "Humanity was first."

"We saw the first god," Louse said.

Barrick materialized next to Tristan. He placed a hand on his shoulder and started to whisper in his ear.

"We have time to discuss this," Sepron said. "Let us make rules for how to conduct ourselves. I, myself, have made mistakes. If we can learn from them and keep this world together, then we may be able to progress further without harm."

The gods began to throw insults at the Eastreans. They exchanged looks between each other. It would be a while before they could all agree on rules for each being to live by.

* * * * *

Odin washed the mud from his hammer. He took some of the remaining leather from his clothing and wrapped it around the hilt to prevent the splintering wood from embedding in his hand.

He thought back on his colossals. How useless they were against Barrick and Arsenal. He would need to have the rest of the giants destroyed so that he could regain some of his power.

He tried to make stones lift into the air and found the effort impossible. He realized he would have to find another way to regain his power. Earth *had* to have other sources of power. Other knowledges that would help him build a new pantheon.

The leather crunched in his hand as he tightened his grip. "One day."

"Trilo," Wallace said. "What happened to Ida?"

The god turned around. "I suppose my message didn't go through. I'm Odin now. I killed the she-beast. Be gone before I do the same to you."

Wallace's heart jumped in his throat. He drew his sword and leveled on top of his shield.

"So be it," Odin said. He brought his hammer up with an oomph. Then Bullio appeared. "Take your friend."

"I do not quit. I am Han Bullio," Bullio said. He braced his giant shield into the mud. Wallace maneuvered behind his friend. He grabbed onto his belt, then let him charge forward.

Bullio pushed his shield into Odin. Even though the god caught it, the force pushed him back.

Feeling the impact, Wallace used the opportunity to climb over Bullio and on top of his shield. He found the god, then drove his sword down. This narrowly missed as Odin pushed out to create enough space for the sword to pass, then rolled to the opposite side, allowing the elephant man to make his advancing slide forward.

Wallace jumped from his friend. His boots dug into the Earth as he forced himself into a stop. He then charged Odin with his horns, catching him under the ribs and digging him into the ground. Odin kicked up and threw the Ram-man up and over into the mud. It caked the side of his legs as it splashed up.

Odin had barely enough time to wipe the muck from his face when Bullio slammed him with his shield and into another headbutt from Wallace. When Wallace went in for another wallop, Odin grabbed him by the horns and threw him to the side.

Bullio slammed him again. This time, Odin caught the shield on its edges. He stuck his feet in the mud and tore it off of and away from the Baptized.

Bullio ducked as the shield was thrown at his head. It went flying miles away from their fight, leaving no room except for Bullio to draw his sword.

Wallace sliced low and Bullio sliced high. When they needed to switch, Wallace would jump to the top of Bullio and dive into their god. With each attack, Odin would block away with his hammer, using all he could to stay away from the Eastrean's weapons.

Left over puddles from the flood splashed as they all collided with expert skill and desperation. At one point, the Baptized thought they had the upper hand before Odin smacked his hammer into the ground, creating a tidal wave of mud that washed them back. Odin thought he would have the upper hand at times but would be quickly put into the defensive as the duo relentlessly attacked any opening he might have.

"Let me be!" Odin demanded. "This can't be a challenging fight for you two."

"This is the only time we might win," Wallace

countered.

Odin screamed and swung his hammer as if he was suddenly surrounded by phantoms. This sent the Baptized back so they could avoid the harsh blows. They knew how heavy the hammer was. Only those with godly strength would be able to wield it. Those on the other end would be its victim.

"Did you never care for your people," Bullio asked through shortened breathing. "We cared for you."

"Why should I have?" Odin said. "It wasn't my job. I was tasked with maintaining the land. The wisdom it held. The people that walked over it came as quickly as the wind could blow them away. It was the power I had that drew people to me. Not my call."

"They had faith in you," Wallace said as he pointed to the god. "Ration had faith in you. *We* had faith in you. Now you are just a victim of the fate you designed."

"Enough!" Odin said. He swung his hammer up, connecting with a boulder next to Bullio, shattering it.

Wallace and Bullio regrouped, then attacked together. Bullio's reflexes told him to slam his shield down. He threw his arm down instead.

Odin swung his hammer up again, this time, catching Bullio perfectly under the neck. The swing was so powerful it took his head off from the shoulders and sent it flying.

"No!" Wallace yelled, charging his god.

Odin grabbed Bullio's trunk in his free hand. Wallace launched through the air, sword above his head. Odin used the opening to drive his hammer up into Wallace's ribcage.

He rolled to the ground. The adrenaline and rage that coursed through his veins blinded him to the pain momentarily. It took everything in him to slide up into a fighting stance. When it all subsided, he fell to his knees, gasping for air. He coughed and blood squirted from his nose and mouth. He looked down at it pouring over his chest.

Odin opened a portal behind him. "Now leave me be." He threw Bullio's head into his chest and both through the portal to the other Eastreans.

The meeting had ended. All gods, including Sepron and Ration, had left. The only souls were Carca, Sark, and Tristan.

"Wallace?" Carca ran to Wallace's side. "What happened? Blazes, Bullio…"

"Trilo," Wallace mustered. "No. Odin. He calls himself Odin now. He did it… We attacked him… we tried to…"

"Don't push yourself," Tristan said. "Let Carca heal you."

He looked at her but her hands were empty. She only stared at the two Baptized with fear and disbelief. "I can't…"

"What do you mean?" Sark asked.

"He's Eastrean," She explained. "I used all of the plants I would need to put Pyre to sleep. That was the last of it. I can fix a few small diseases. A bad rash for us even. But this? Nothing on Earth has enough strength to fix Eastrean bones."

"No…" Tristan said. "Lanta. Did you find Lanta?"

"Dead… Mal has her... Coming to you…" Wallace's eyes drifted up and passed the Immortals.

The night moon stood over him. He held his scythe in one hand, and a loaf of bread in another. "Time to go to the Interworlds, friend."

Ida Lanta stood next to him. She appeared as though she was never injured. She cried through a smile down to her friend. "Come on, Nathanial. You silly fool. You never would have made it far without me."

Wallace smiled up at them. He reached out and took Lanta's hand. "Ida. I tried. I tried…I needed you too."

The Immortals looked where Wallace was talking but saw nothing. They knew what was happening. They knew when their death was there and what to expect. They wept for their friend. The friend who protected them, who laughed with them, and lived with them. He who was struggling to take his final breaths as his own collapsed lungs betrayed him.

"I know you did," Ida said. "I'm so proud of you."

"Take your time together," Death said. "I won't rush us Eastreans."

"I begged him to let me wait for you," Lanta continued "You fought so hard and I'm so proud of you. Come with me now. Accompany me to our last adventure."

"I'd like that, Ida," Wallace said. His soul stood up from his body. Lanta helped him up and propped him up on her shoulders. When he could stand and realized it wasn't difficult to breath. He stood up straight. He took Ida's hand in his. "I was Nathanial Wallace. A soldier of the Baptized in Fire. I was a good friend. A fierce fighter. A loving family member. I cherished my friendship with Ida Lanta above all."

Ida smiled up at him. She climbed on his shoulders and between his horns like she used to do. "I was Ida Lanta. A devout follower of Ration and Sepron. I was a soldier of the Baptized in Fire. I was a good friend. A great warrior. I stood by my friend, Nathanial Wallace, above all."

As they followed Death into the afterlife. They told their favorite stories from their lives together. Their fondness for the adventure filling the swirling blue air.

* * * * *

1 week later

Tristan stood outside of Reality's Bend. Its dark clouds tossed and turned. It hovered over its designated position. He did as the Immortal of Reality instructed and knocked.

Even though it appeared to be a formless cloud, the sound of wood echoed within. After a few moments, Barrick Teal opened the door. He hadn't slept in days. A luxury he felt he would never get back. His disheveled hair was matted to one side and ruffled on the other.

"Thank you for coming," he said. "Follow me."

They walked through the long corridor to the last door as Tristan carried a large clanking sack over his shoulder. He would occasionally adjust it as he wondered what was behind each door.

"What do you think of the war?" Tristan asked. "You took a larger toll than most of us. I didn't think it was possible but I saw one of our own die in front of my eyes."

"Wars will happen," Barrick said. He reached for the door and twisted the doorknob.

"Interesting method," Tristan said.

"I pulled it from Arsenal's history."

Green glowing threads decorated the walls around them. A statue in the shape of Barrick was I the center of the room awaiting its purpose.

Barrick motioned. Tristan drug his bag over to the statue and started to piece the armor together with delicate precision. He then took out a double-sided sword with a short hilt designed for disarming and rested it on the side.

When he was finished, he asked, "What now?" as he slapped his knees.

"Stand back," Barrick said.

The Immortal did so. Barrick then grabbed the strings and pulled. The myriad of stitches fell from the walls. They spiraled as each layer fell onto the armor and sword, disappearing into them. The Eastrean words, *Pyeplo Glose Vantur*, appeared.

"God Killer Armor?" Tristan asked. "Should such a thing exist."

"All of our gods did great damage last week," Barrick said. "Even with the God Pact in place, it doesn't hurt to have a precaution."

Tristan nodded. "I won't say anything. Just don't use it if you don't have to."

"I won't. That's why I asked you to make that other set." Barrick motioned for the bag.

From it, Tristan brought out another set of leather armor. It was decorated with images of bees and flowers and rivers. He fixed each peace to Barrick.

"It's beautiful," Barrick said. "Thank you."

"One more thing," Tristan said. He pulled an Eastrean battle axe. It was shorter than it usually would be though it should be considering the source. "I took the hilt from Trilo…Odin's hammer. Then I melted some of Bullio's armor down for the head. There isn't much of our materials left so I'm trying to make do where I can."

"It's perfect. Thank you." Barrick took the axe. It fused to his soul like his other axe did. It glowed brightly and out the door.

As the second axe of reality claimed its owner, the

door to Reality's Bend shut to all outsiders. Destined to protect the secrets inside.

An Immortal Tale

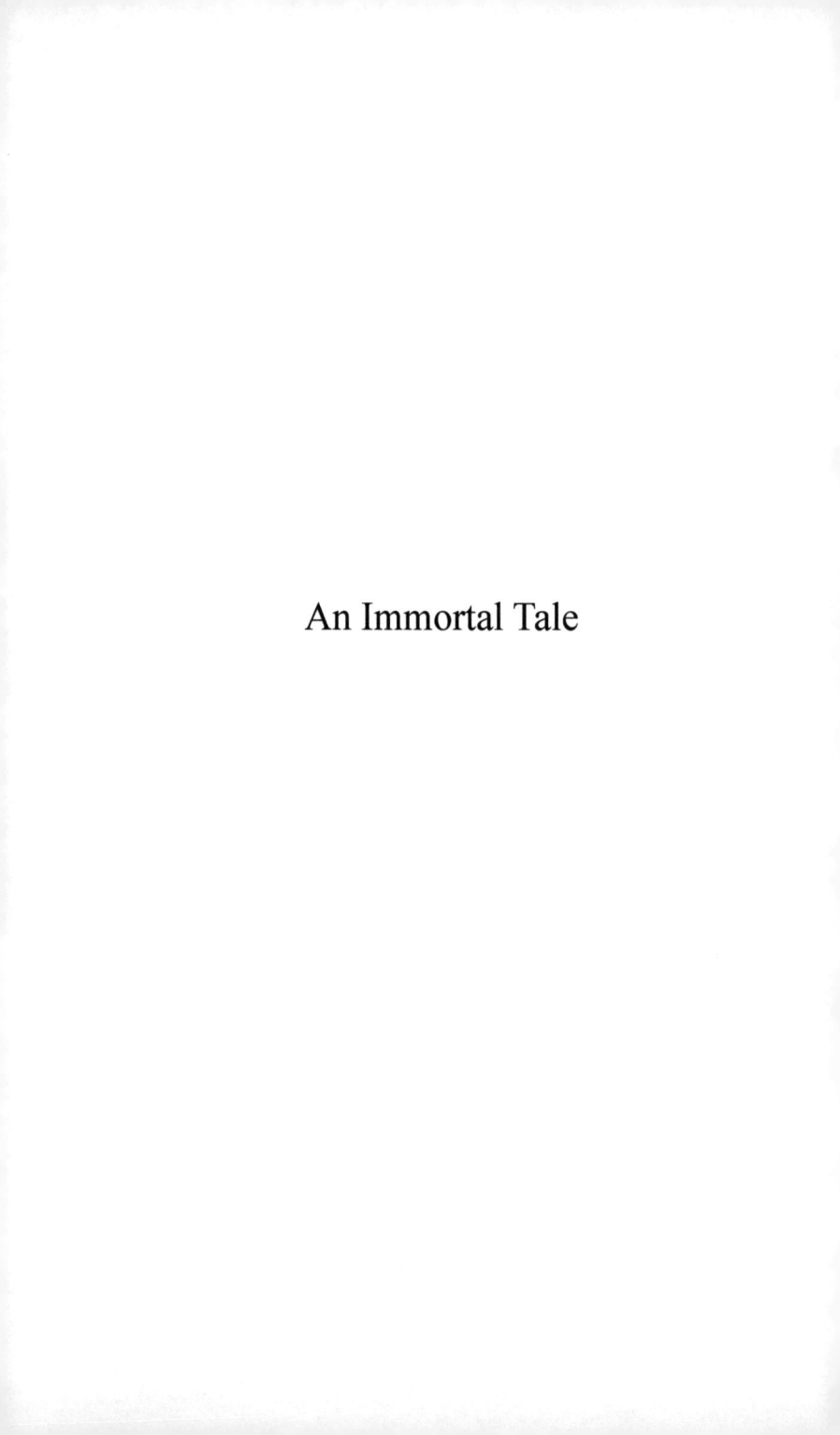

The Book

Kataract made port over the northern most point of the horn of Africa. The waves beckoned to him like dogs ready for their next command. He peered over The Reacher at them. The sounds of their song lulled him to the point that he allowed himself to close his eyes.

Asha flew down next to him from her post. She stared at his content expression. She wondered what made him so calm. Especially so soon after the fight they just had.

He opened his eyes and turned to his second in command. "Amazing how quiet the world is. The currents tell me they carried a man and woman here after the war. Cities were swept away. Almost like Barrick did with War God's people."

"Isn't there only one current?" Asha asked.

"Yes and no," Kataract said. "Look closer. I showed

you how to see the way they flow. But now look into that one there. The different swirls that talk to each other. Tell each other where to go. See how they are different shades of colors. A painting almost. One to be lost in. There."

Asha tried but found herself lacking in the skill. She didn't doubt her captain. She'd sailed with him for several thousand years at that point and the way he read the currents in seamless dedication told of the mind that could have very well created them. She knew better after meeting the Eastrean gods, however. After seeing them and their strength, there was no doubt in her mind who created the world they lived on.

"Kataract!" the prophet called from the captain's quarters. Chris Louse had asked to travel with the crew on her quest to understand the visions presented to her. She had taken the time to study under prophets and oracles alike to understand her abilities. "I have it."

"That's wonderful, Louse," Kataract said with the foggiest idea as to what she meant. "Do show me."

Asha rolled her eyes at his blind kindness. She started to follow him to the quarters but was stopped.

"Not you," Louse said with a hand in the air. "This is an Eastrean matter. Please don't take offense. I don't even know what to make of it."

"Must be something big," Kataract laughed. He patted the Kurara on her back. "I'll call if I need anything."

Asha nodded then returned to her post.

On the floor were scattered sheets that Kataract found difficult to navigate with his massive feet. Louse on the other hand danced around them like she made strings to follow.

"See, Kataract, see!" She pointed at the sheets. Her eyes expected him to put the scene together himself.

Gods of the Flood

Kataract gave a defeated laugh, "I'm sorry, Louse. I'm afraid you are going to have to spell it out for me."

"Us," Louse rubbed her palms into eyes to try to shake exhaustion. "It's us. Not just us. There are others. They're familiar somehow. We've met them, but haven't. Different versions of them. This is our history, Kataract. Some of it anyways."

"You wrote it down?" Kataract said. He picked up a sheet and read the Eastrean. He noticed his name in the lines. They told of the meeting to take down Graphite before the end of Eastrea. "You weren't there..."

"It's our stories," Louse said. She scrambled to gather all of the sheets in the order only she knew. Almost a thousand pages came together in slow succession leaving Kataract to watch.

Louse took a slab of hide. She cut it to the appropriate length. She heated a knife until it was glowing. She then etched into it with smoke rolling off into her eyes. When done, she showed her work to Kataract.

"Severteen Borum?" he said. "The God Fall. Louse, I'm sorry but I don't know the point of all of this."

Louse let out a large grunt. She pulled out a needle to which she put to the hide and paper until she had formed a large book. She then flipped it open to her desired page.

"Read, Kataract," Louse said. She pointed at a specific place on the page to draw his attention in.

He read aloud, "Read, Kataract. Louse said..."

"Starting to peace it together?" Louse asked, hand still on the page.

The flying captain took the book into his arms. He flipped through the pages until the end. "You left room for more?"

"No, it's complete," she said through crossed arms. Kataract showed her. She frowned at the pages. "No. It was here. I swear it. That's Barrick's section. He met a young god. Helped you. Helped Ration. There was a war. Blazes with these visions. They get so blurred after I see them."

She stepped away to mutter to herself.

Kataract thumbed through the pages. He skipped to the Flood War. He read Barrick's sections. What had happened to Neith. How alone he seemed after. He was grateful Arsenal was there but wished he had known about the weight he carried.

He started to skip ahead and found himself wanting to look away. He felt as though knowing his future was taboo. Then he noticed something about the stories.

"Louse," he said. The Baptized in Fire broke away from her rambling. "These are just stories. Where is the rest of it. Eastrea. There are whole histories missing."

"I only saw what was important," Louse said. "It was up to us to remember Eastrea. *We* have to tell those stories. This book, the Seventeen Borum, it is the important things. How we failed. How we survived. I tried to warn Ration. I tried to tell him but I think he knew."

"What?" Kataract said. He had his suspicions about his god but now he was starting to gather the truth.

"Ration knows everything," Louse explained. "You didn't know that? He is powerless to stop it. If he tries, Pyre makes sure those things happen anyways. That's why he made Barrick and Arsenal. They slow Pyre."

"I didn't know," Kataract said. He flipped through the book some more. He wasn't reading. It was more nervous actions taking over his mind as he thought about the nature of his god. *Some things have to happen. And happen exactly?*

He stopped when he noticed a name start to appear in the back half of the book. He turned to the first occurrence. He showed it to Louse. "Who is Ethan Pyre?"

Gods of the Flood

The Worshipped Around Reality's Bend
Book 3
Immortals of Earth

Spring 2025

Ration has little choice but to expand. After losing so many in the Flood War, he reaches out to Barrick to find new Immortals. Those heroes from history soon fill the ranks of the New Eastrean Immortals. As their ranks grow, the gods of the world take notice and set out to push against what they see as a potential threat. All the while ignoring the new era the Eastreans are about to bring.

Like the series and want to stay updated? Follow the QR code below or visit clintbakerstories.com.

At these places you can see all related writing, interviews, and more.